D0822788

PEOPLE LIKE US

People Like Us

SHORT STORIES

Javier Valdés

Translated by Stephen Lytle

ATRIA BOOKS

New York   London   Toronto   Sydney

ATRIA BOOKS
1230 Avenue of the Americas
New York, NY 10020

This book is a work of fiction. Names, characters, places and incidents are products of the author's imagination or are used fictitiously. Any resemblance to actual events or locales or persons, living or dead, is entirely coincidental.

Copyright © 1997 by Javier Valdés
Copyright © 1997 by Hoja Casa Editorial, S.A. de C.V.

English translation copyright © 2006 by Javier Valdés
Translated by Stephen A. Lytle

Originally published in Spanish in 1997 by Hoja Casa Editorial,
S.A. de C.V. as *Cuentos para baño*

All rights reserved, including the right to reproduce
this book or portions thereof in any form whatsoever.
For information address Atria Books, 1230 Avenue
of the Americas, New York, NY 10020

Library of Congress Cataloging-in-Publication Data

Valdés, Javier (Valdés Abascal).
[Cuentos para baño. English]
People like us / Javier Valdés ; translated by Stephen Lytle.
p. cm.
I. Lytle, Stephen A.   II. Title.
PQ7298.432.A35C8413 2006
863'.7—dc22   2005057180

ISBN-13: 978-0-7432-8646-6
ISBN-10:   0-7432-8646-4

First Atria Books trade paperback edition June 2006

1   3   5   7   9   10   8   6   4   2

ATRIA BOOKS is a trademark of Simon & Schuster, Inc.

Manufactured in the United States of America

For information about special discounts for bulk purchases,
please contact Simon & Schuster Special Sales at
1-800-456-6798 or business@simonandschuster.com.

For Laura

CONTENTS

PEOPLE LIKE US

PEOPLE LIKE US

Gold is cash and love is a worthless check.

Ana laura and I decided to spend part of the winter in the mountains. After weighing all the possibilities, we were leaning toward renting a house. Although we wouldn't have the conveniences of a hotel, we wouldn't have the inconveniences either, and it would cost about a third as much.

Besides, we would have the peace and quiet we both needed to be able to work. Ana Laura had to correct six texts that her editor was to publish in February and I had to finish more than twelve stories, which I had started some time ago and which would serve to pay a good portion of my not-unsubstantial debts.

So that's what we ended up doing. We loaded my tiny car with food and equipment for our pending work and then set off for our temporary paradise on earth.

The route to the mountains was rife with splendid aromas and scenes. The birds were singing as if it were the last day of their lives, and the painting that nature was unfolding impressed us beyond measure.

We stopped at a scenic overlook along the highway to better appreciate the countryside.

Although many of the trees were leafless, others still glowed a stunning dark green. The ground was carpeted with leaves, forming a mosaic in several shades of brown. In the distance, the tallest peaks were enveloped in snow and clouds that seemed to kiss them.

The air was cold, but pleasant.

We smoked a cigarette in silence as we contemplated the landscape.

"Which way is the house?" asked Ana Laura.

I thought a moment and then pointed to a spot between two low mountains. "Over there," I replied.

Her gaze followed my finger to the horizon.

"Okay then, let's go. This is beautiful, but I wouldn't want to spend the night here."

We got back in the Volkswagen, which soon began to show signs of fatigue as we started the steepest part of the ascent, but German technology ultimately prevailed and the small car successfully scaled the slopes.

We finally arrived at the house around six o'clock, and by then it was much colder.

The house was a real icebox and felt even colder than outside, but the fireplace was stacked with dry wood and it didn't take us long to get a good fire going.

We huddled in front of the flames until our bones warmed up again. Then we made several trips to the car to get our bags, Ana Laura's laptop, and my word processor.

Once this was done, we set about inspecting the house.

It was a small structure, fairly old, but immaculately maintained. There was a pleasant living room, a dining room, a big kitchen—which seemed overly large for the tiny house—and a very cozy bedroom with another fireplace, which Ana Laura immediately lit.

We poured ourselves drinks and ate cheese and pâté. After eating, we unpacked, stoked the fireplaces, and went to bed. The drive had been tiring, not just for the Volkswagen, but for us too, and the cold made us burrow under the heavy down comforter.

The next day we each began our respective work. The mountain air made me feel wonderful and I finished a story that I'd been stuck on for six months. Ana Laura, on the other hand, worked for a few hours and then started poking around the house. By five o'clock she had already drunk more than half a bottle of vodka. At eight I had to carry her to bed, because she had fallen asleep in front of the fire.

Several days passed in similar fashion. Since she wasn't drunk all the time, Ana Laura soon realized that it had been a mistake for us to cloister ourselves in such a remote part of the world. The poor woman couldn't work and went out for long walks in the forest. She took the car to town several times to buy groceries—and vodka. Meanwhile, I quickly finished one story after another. I felt like a freshly uncorked bottle of sparkling wine, and sentence after sentence bubbled out with an ease I had never known before.

Ana Laura's laptop remained solitary and inactive, as if it were nothing more than a prop.

I knew very well that Ana Laura was dying to go back to the city or someplace more lively, but she didn't say a word. She wore her boredom stoically.

One afternoon, at the height of her boredom, she discovered a door to the attic. It had been sealed, but no seal can withstand feminine curiosity, and Ana Laura launched an exploration of the space, with the aid of a flashlight she brought in from the car.

At dinnertime she showed me something interesting that she had found earlier that afternoon. It was an old notebook with drawings of the house we were occupying, and it showed in precise sequence how it had been built, from the empty lot to the completed structure. There were details on the foundation, the construction of the walls, even the roof.

Each drawing carried a date at the bottom of the page. The house had been completed over a century ago.

"What do you think?" Ana Laura asked as she closed the notebook.

"Excellent artist."

We didn't talk about it any more that night.

From that point on, my girlfriend's boredom completely disappeared. She spent the days studying the drawings in the old notebook. She seemed hypnotized by them and spent hours poring over each one, as if it were from a collection of old Flemish masters. Ana Laura stopped drinking vodka and walking in the woods and hardly ate anything. It was almost as if she were under a spell of some kind.

The third day after her find in the attic, she interrupted my work. "Look at this!"

She indicated a particular portion of a drawing. I had no idea what she was trying to show me. "What is it?"

"It looks like some sort of cellar."

Sure enough, the drawing indicated a large opening right beneath the kitchen floor. "It's probably just a cistern," I said, trying to get back to work.

"I don't think so," she insisted. "There's plenty of water around here. And besides, there's a well a few yards from the house. Why build a cistern? There's something else," she added, slightly raising one of her beautiful eyebrows. "I already examined the kitchen floor and there's no opening."

"So?" I asked disinterestedly as I lit a cigarette.

"It could be a secret hiding place. Maybe there's treasure inside. Can you imagine?"

By now my rhythm had been totally broken, so I began to pay closer attention to what my beautiful companion was suggesting.

"You said there's no opening in the kitchen floor?"

"Look for yourself."

I went into the kitchen with the open notebook in my hands and stood over where I figured the hole should be.

There was nothing. But I did notice the stone floor covering the kitchen floor was not the same as in the drawing of the half-completed house.

This stuff looked newer.

"It's not the same floor," I said, looking distractedly at the tips of my boots.

Ana Laura seemed disappointed when she saw what I meant.

Just to make my lady happy, I tapped all over the kitchen floor with the heels of my boots. It was as solid as a rock.

"Look, Ana Laura, it must have been some sort of storage cellar. There was probably no need for it anymore, and when they changed the kitchen floor, the new owners simply filled in the hole."

"I guess you're right, but it was an interesting idea, wasn't it?" She had the look of a little girl who had been scolded.

The next morning, I found Ana Laura lying on the kitchen floor, inspecting it inch by inch.

I had other things to do, so I didn't pay any attention. If she wanted to spend the day searching for clues to a nonexistent treasure, that was her choice. I was going to get my work done.

Next time I looked, I saw she'd given up her scrutiny of the kitchen floor and gone back up to the attic.

A few hours later she came down covered with dust and carrying a roll of very old paper.

Without saying a word she unrolled it in front of me, covering my word processor.

It was a well-designed construction project. Drawn in sepia ink, it appeared to be the original plan for the house. There was no doubt that it was the work of a consummate artist.

And there it was again—the cellar beneath the kitchen, clearly delineated with a dotted line, which indicated that it was underground.

Now I had to take Ana Laura seriously.

If it were some sort of storage space and had been sealed, we wouldn't lose anything by looking around a little, if only to please Ana Laura.

The next day we went into town. There was no office for the regulation or registration of private construction projects, but we were told that we could find information on local buildings at the public library.

The matronly woman who attended us in the library was colder than the morning, and it took several minutes to convince her we weren't planning to rob the place. Finally, after glaring at us fixedly, she led us to the reading room, ordering us to sit down and indicating that we were to remain silent by putting a finger to her lips. Neither Ana Laura nor I had said a word, but the ugly harpy seemed to enjoy treating us like a couple of schoolkids.

She disappeared for what seemed like an eternity and then reappeared carrying a very large book and two other smaller volumes, all quite old.

She opened the large book on one of the tables and wordlessly signaled that it contained what she thought we were looking for. Then, speaking in a very low voice—which was ridiculous, because there was no one else in the room—she told us that we would find additional information in the two smaller books. She warned us to be careful with the material, since it was very valuable. She returned after a few minutes to stare at us again, and finally disappeared in the direction of her desk.

Laughing, Ana Laura turned to look at me and whispered, "You better behave yourself if you don't want the teacher to expel you from school."

I had to control myself to keep from laughing out loud. Not that the joke was so funny, but the tension in that place made it seem hilarious.

Stifling our laughter, we began looking through the large volume. It had no title but contained copies of sketches from various construction projects, both in town and in the outlying areas. The drawings were accompanied by brief descriptions of the projects and sets of plans.

We found our house on one of the center pages. The drawing was identical to the one Ana Laura had found in the attic. It looked like a photocopy.

The description of the house didn't give any new information but merely provided technical details.

We looked at several similar projects, and none had a cellar.

Ana Laura interrupted my musing. "If it's an ordinary building, why is it included in the town's book?"

Without waiting for a response, which would have consisted of an impotent shrugging of my shoulders, she began leafing through one of the smaller tomes. I did the same with the other one.

The book I was looking at described several homes in the area along with their histories.

The house that we were occupying had the unique characteristic of having been designed and drawn by a prodigal son of the region, who had been an exquisite and impeccable artist.

"Look at this!" shouted Ana Laura.

I barely had a chance to look at the book when a chilling voice sounded, causing the hair on my neck to stand on end.

"If you don't intend to keep quiet, you'd better leave."

It was the librarian. She was visibly upset and threatened us with a long, crooked index finger.

"Please excuse us," said Ana Laura, in a very low, sweet voice.

"That's the last warning. Next time, we will be forced to suspend your privileges."

The old witch spoke in the plural, as if we were in the main branch of the New York Public Library and not in a little hole in some remote corner of the mountains.

Fortunately she returned to her desk and Ana Laura pointed with a manicured finger to the section of the book that she had been reading.

It described the construction of the foundation of our house, focusing principally on its design. It seemed that the owner of the house had hired the best architect in the area to design a hiding place. Not a simple basement, rather a carefully planned refuge in which the owner could protect himself in case of war.

So that was what made the house special and why it was listed in the books.

Ana Laura politely asked the librarian if we could make photocopies of the plans and drawings, but the witch vehemently refused, arguing that the copying machine was for the exclusive use of the library and not for "rowdy tourists."

"Could you lend us the book then to make copies somewhere else?" she asked.

"Certainly not!" she exclaimed loftily. She would never place the village's treasures in the hands of people like us!

"What do you suggest then?" I asked, amused, recalling my high school days.

"I suggest that you leave. You are not welcome here."

Saying this, she grabbed the three books and proceeded to put them back on the shelves, effectively ending the conversation.

Once we were back in the street, the cold air hit us with such force that we sought refuge in a café.

A string of bells rang as we opened the door, and the scent of fresh-baked bread and coffee comfortingly enveloped us. A cozy fire burned in a fireplace along one wall.

An obese old man, wearing a large white apron and with a kind face, approached to take our order. His face—especially his nose—showed signs of a long, useless battle against alcohol abuse, but he was very attentive and agreeable.

We ordered coffee and a couple of brandies—to warm up.

Only two other tables were occupied, and a solitary man smoked a pipe at the bar in front of a steaming cup of coffee.

The fat man brought over what we had ordered. "Tourists?" he asked with a scratchy voice.

After the experience we had suffered in the library, I hesitated to respond.

"We rented a house outside of town. We're actually here to work. We're writers." Ana Laura had spoken and was now flashing one of her adorable smiles.

The man smiled back warmly, exposing a large, black space where there had once been teeth.

"Welcome!" he exclaimed. Without another word he went back behind the bar and began polishing an interminable supply of glasses and cups.

Like the sugar in our coffee, his behavior rapidly dissipated the bitterness caused by the librarian. After a few minutes, we ordered more brandy. The coffee was very strong, but delicious.

The smiling man served us again. "These are on the house," he said, helping himself to a glass too.

Ana Laura invited him to sit with us, and he eagerly accepted.

His name was Guillermo.

"Which house is it that you rented?" he asked after a few minutes of chatting.

We described the house.

"Ah! The Bernabeu house."

"Do you know it?" asked Ana Laura, with a childlike smile of surprise.

"Everyone in town knows it. My father used to say that the owner was a half-crazy Frenchman. He spent his life worrying about wars and invasions. . . ."

He took a sip of his brandy and, after wiping his lips on the back of his hand, continued. "They say he was obsessed with war. He hired one of our best boys to make him a house with a hiding place. He said they weren't going to get him so easily."

Just then, one of the townspeople called out to the barman, demanding to be served.

"I'll be right back," he said, flooding the air with the dense smell of alcohol.

A few minutes later he returned to our table but didn't sit down. Instead, he crossed his arms and asked, "What were we talking about?"

"You were saying that Bernabeu was obsessed with war," replied Ana Laura, interestedly.

"Ah! Yes! And invasions! It seems that his grandfather had served in Napoleon's army and must have told the poor boy too many awful stories about the war when he was a child."

"But, if everyone knew that he had a hiding place, that didn't give him any advantage, did it?" asked Ana Laura.

Guillermo put his index finger to his temple and made a few circling motions, indicating craziness.

"What happened to him?" I asked.

"To Bernabeu? No one knows for sure. I think after he finished the house he got married and left town."

"Has anyone been in the hiding place?" demanded Laura.

"No one. After the Frenchman left and before the town took over the abandoned house, a lot of curious folks tried to figure out how to get into the cellar. I guess they thought there was something of value down there. But it seems that Bernabeu did a good job. No one has been able to find a way in."

The man went back behind the bar and resumed his polishing.

We remained silent for a few minutes.

"We have to get into that cellar. There must be something there," said Ana Laura.

"Take it easy, my dear. Before we destroy the house, we should look for an entrance to the hiding place. There must be one," I said, hardly convinced.

We paid our bill and went out into the cold street again.

Once in the car, we headed back to the house in silence. The tale of the paranoid Bernabeu stayed on my mind, and I thought I might be able to write a good story about it. Or better still, if we were somehow able to get into the cellar, a story wouldn't be enough. More likely a novel, no matter what we actually found there. What else is a writer's imagination for?

Maybe there wasn't anything of value buried there, but, if I could write an interesting novel, that might turn out to be a small treasure in itself.

The house was very cold when we arrived, and Ana Laura stoked the fires in both fireplaces.

Although it was still early, the brandy had made us quite warm, and so we had several glasses of vodka before sprawling out on the sofa in front of the fireplace in the living room. We watched the flames devour the dry wood for a long time.

"What do you think we should do?" Ana Laura said after a while.

"We could look for some kind of access to the cellar, if it still exists."

She rewarded me with the best smile in her repertoire and replied, "Let's get to work."

Finishing off the rest of the vodka in our glasses, we divided up the labor.

I was to explore the kitchen, the bathroom, and the bedroom; Ana Laura, the living room, the dining room, and, just in case, the attic.

We spent hours searching every corner, every nook. If someone had been watching us, he would have thought that we were completely insane, or else that we were rehearsing an Ionesco play.

We crawled on the floor like cockroaches. We took pictures and mirrors off the walls. We felt every orifice and every panel of wood looking for buttons and trick levers.

Nothing.

By seven o'clock we were completely exhausted and starving. We hadn't discovered anything more substantial than a few spiderwebs and a lot of dust.

The air was filled with a sense of failure and disillusion.

We ate a dinner of cold turkey and drank a bottle of white wine. We stoked the fires again and went to bed.

We weren't in a mood conducive to sexual activity and were both soon profoundly asleep.

. . . I was in Bernabeu's hiding place. It was a small but well-organized room. I saw several large cushions, some blankets, and cans of food piled on the floor. Two small containers, about five gallons each, held water. Farther back there were several boxes con-

taining dried meats, crackers, jars of conserved fruits, and a burlap bag filled with walnuts, another filled with hazelnuts, and another filled with pine nuts.

I walked around the room, and, although it was completely dark, I could see everything clearly. The place was very tidy, as if someone had just cleaned it. On top of a wooden box of dried fish there was a sepia photograph. I took it in my hands. It was very old and showed a newly married couple posing soberly for the camera. When I looked more carefully, I couldn't help being alarmed. It was a photograph of Ana Laura and me! . . .

I awakened drenched with sweat. It took two minutes to convince myself that it had just been a dream—a nightmare—produced by the obsessive search we had carried out the previous afternoon.

I went to the kitchen, turned on the light, and lit a cigarette. The bottle of vodka was within reach, so I helped myself to a drink.

Ana Laura and I were obsessing, that was all. If there was a cellar, it had simply been sealed off long ago. Period. I had no reason to keep following my beautiful companion's quest. The subject was closed.

The next day I would clear it up with Ana Laura and get back to work. Back to what would feed me and pay for my share of this house. Bernabeu and his damned paranoia could just go to hell.

I didn't need any more nightmares like that one. . . .

Suddenly I heard a noise. I froze. Not only could I hear but I could feel footsteps approaching.

For a moment I ceased breathing and my heart stopped.

The glass of vodka in my hand fused with my fingers as if it were a part of my body. For a stupid second I gazed at the transparent liquid. As still as a frozen pool.

Now what? Bernabeu's ghost? Some soul in anguish?

I closed my eyes, expecting the worst. When I opened them again I jumped with fright, letting go of the glass, which shattered in slow motion on the stone floor.

A blond ghost dressed in white was standing in front of me.

"Will you pour me one?" said Ana Laura, her face screwed up. "I've had a terrible nightmare."

Feigning interest, I served her a little vodka in a glass. I cleared my throat, like a chicken in the slaughterhouse, and, trying to sound calm, asked what she had dreamed.

Ana Laura described her dream down to the last detail.

I felt as if someone had run a piece of ice down my spine.

Ana Laura's dream was identical to mine.

"It must be exhaustion," I said, trying to sound like I believed myself.

She swallowed her drink in one gulp and, giving me a kiss on the cheek, said, "Of course!" Then she went off to bed.

I drank several more glasses of vodka before I found sufficient courage to return to bed, and the unsettling dreamworld.

The next day I awoke with an unbearable headache, feeling as if a sword had been stuck from my forehead all the way down through my neck. I looked at my watch. It was past one-thirty in the afternoon.

Holding my head with both hands to prevent unnecessary pain, I went to the kitchen and took four aspirin.

Ana Laura was nowhere in sight. I went into the bathroom

and took a steaming shower, gradually lowering the temperature until I could no longer stand the freezing water. Then I ran back to the bedroom.

The sword had disappeared but had left behind a dull hammering in my skull. I got dressed but didn't have enough strength to do anything, so I lay down on the bed and closed my eyes, wishing I hadn't drunk so much vodka the night before.

> . . . *I was in the cellar in front of a large metal door. I tried to open it, but I couldn't.*
>
> *I frantically kicked it with all my strength. It wouldn't budge. A gripping panic overcame me. I wasn't going to be able to get out of the damned hiding place.*
>
> *I began to hear faint shouts calling my name, over and over.*
>
> *It was Ana Laura. I couldn't tell where her voice was coming from, but I could hear it clearly now. . . .*

It was already dark outside when I opened my eyes. Only a light pain remained in my temples from my earlier hangover. The house was dark, so I turned on the lights as I called for Ana Laura.

She didn't answer. I looked all over the house.

There was no sign of her. There weren't even dirty dishes or glasses in the kitchen.

Everything was just as I had left it earlier that afternoon.

I went outside to see if she had taken the car.

The Volkswagen was still where we had parked the night before. It was freezing outside, so I went back into the house and tried to calm myself. She had to be somewhere nearby.

But where? Was she out walking in the woods in the dark? Maybe she had walked into town? Not likely—it was almost two miles away.

Soon I began to feel a tremendous emptiness in the pit of my stomach, and my cheeks were burning.

Just as in my dream, I was being overcome by an unbearable panic attack.

Though I knew better, I poured myself a drink, this time choosing scotch. The memory of the hellish vodka hangover was still fresh in my mind.

What should I do now? Go look for her in town?

Had she seen that I was sleeping so long and decided to run some errands? Without the car? Without leaving a note?

I emptied the glass of scotch in one gulp and immediately poured myself another. I was trying to control myself . . . unsuccessfully.

I emptied that glass too. Then I put on a jacket and went out to the car. I was going to go into town to look for her. She had to be there.

Just before I got into the car, I heard—just like in my dream—a voice calling my name in the distance.

Was I hallucinating?

Where was the voice coming from?

I looked in the glove compartment for the flashlight, but it wasn't there. Then I remembered that Ana Laura had used it to search the attic.

The shouts were further apart now, but I could hear them more clearly. They were coming from behind the house.

I turned on the car's headlights. They didn't help much, but it was better than nothing.

I lumbered up the small hill behind the house to where the shouts seemed to be originating.

By now I was sure I wasn't hallucinating. Ana Laura must be in danger!

It had snowed the night before, and the ground was very slippery. I was wearing city shoes, so every two steps I had to perform acrobatics so as not to fall on my face. That, and my girlfriend's shouting, made me think that maybe I was having another nightmare. But when I slipped and fell, smashing my face against a rock, I knew I wasn't dreaming.

I actually saw stars, and my right cheek burned with pain. There is no worse injury than one sustained in freezing temperatures. I got up as best I could and tried to reorient myself.

The Volkswagen's headlights were by now only dim, and since I was directly behind the house, it blocked their light. The curtains in the kitchen windows, which looked out at where I was, were closed and only gave off a faint light around the edges.

All I could hear was the howling of the wind as it whispered through the trees in the dark forest.

Was that all it had been?

A trick of nature?

Then suddenly, from a few yards ahead of me, I clearly heard Ana Laura's voice, followed by a sharp echo.

I felt my way toward the source of the sounds.

Now her voice was only two or three yards away, but it sounded heavy and distorted, as if she had placed a cardboard tube in front of her mouth before shouting.

My eyes had adjusted somewhat to the darkness at this point, and I could make out a shadow in the distance with an arch above it. . . . It was the well!

Sweating heavily, and with my face still numb from the fall, I grabbed the edge of the well and again clearly heard Ana Laura's voice, calling for help from inside the well.

"Ana Laura?"

"Here . . . down here . . . ," she said wearily.

"What happened? Are you okay?"

"I feel like shit and I'm freezing to death. Get me out of here!"

"Okay. Calm down! Let me get the flashlight."

"I have the flashlight down here, but the batteries have run out."

Ana Laura's voice sounded hollow.

"How deep is it?"

"About nine feet. Hurry up! I'm standing in freezing water, and it's ridiculously cold down here."

I tried to see the bottom but couldn't.

"Hang on just a little longer," I told her while I took off my jacket and threw it inside. "Here's this. Don't worry. I'm going to the house to find something to get you out with."

"Hurry up!"

My eyes were fully adjusted to the darkness now, and I cautiously returned to the house. I was not eager to fall again. I went to the kitchen door, which was the nearest entrance to the house. It wouldn't open. Then I remembered that the door had been locked from the inside.

I made my way around the corner of the house to the car and the degree of safety that the headlights afforded.

Finally I reached the front door. The first thing I did was open the kitchen curtains.

They didn't provide much light, but it was something.

Then I looked around for something I could use to get Ana Laura out of this mess she'd gotten herself into.

Even if there had been a good rope—which there wasn't—and I could somehow have secured it to the arch above the well, it wouldn't be easy for her to grip the rope with her frozen fingers and scale the walls; that happens only in movies.

Suddenly, I thought of something. I went to the door that led to the attic and lowered the wooden ladder leading up to it. I tried to pull it off the door where it was attached.

Impossible.

I went to look for a hatchet I had seen near the car and had used to cut firewood.

After several chops with the hatchet, the ladder gave way.

It wasn't very long, only a few yards, but it would help.

I took the ladder and carried it out the kitchen door.

"Here I am, my love," I said, feeling incredibly stupid.

"We can talk later. Just get me out of here," she yelled, then more quietly, "idiot."

"I'm going to hand a ladder down. Be careful, I don't want to hit your head."

"That's all I need. Go ahead, lower it down!"

I eased the ladder down with its rough ends first, thinking they'd offer some resistance against the slippery floor.

I leaned way over the edge of the well but still couldn't feel the ladder coming into contact with anything.

"Try to grip it, Annie, but carefully, because—"

"Owww!"

"—it has splinters on the end."

I felt her grab the ladder, and then after some huffing and

foul language, her head appeared out of the darkness at the rim of the well.

Without speaking, I helped her out, and we went quickly back to the house.

I took her into the bedroom, covered her with the down comforter, and poured her a large glass of brandy. Ana Laura was shivering uncontrollably, and her lips were a color somewhere between purple and blue. I made her drink all the brandy.

My first thought had been to put her into a steaming shower, but that might have killed her or at the least ruptured a bunch of blood vessels. The risk of pneumonia seemed the lesser of two evils.

When she finished the brandy, she breathed deeply and started coughing. Good, I thought. That would help her warm up.

I built up the fire in the bedroom until it roared, then went into the bathroom and wet a towel with hot water. I squeezed out the excess water, went back to Ana Laura, and removed her clothing. Her skin was covered with goose bumps, and her teeth chattered noisily. I rubbed her body roughly with the hot towel. I went back to heat up the towel again and repeated the process several times. She was starting to look better, thanks to the fireplace, which by now had warmed up the room quite nicely.

Soon she stopped trembling and shivering and seemed to relax a little.

I poured her more brandy, and she drank it eagerly.

I got out some flannel pajamas and put them as close to

the fire as I dared. When they were hot, I helped Ana Laura put them on. She was feeling better by the minute.

When she finished her third glass of brandy, the color had returned to her face and her cheeks were rosy again.

I left her alone for a few minutes to go make some coffee.

It was very hot, so she had to drink it in tiny sips. By the time she finished her coffee, she was a new person.

I was dying of curiosity but didn't want to grill her yet about how she'd ended up at the bottom of the well. After I'd covered her with the blankets and put more wood on the fire, I asked her if she wanted anything else. She said no.

I gave her a light kiss on the lips and left the room, closing the door behind me. I barely made out a weak "thank you" from behind the door.

Since I had spent the whole day sleeping, the last thing I wanted to do was go back to bed, so I tried to write a little. The words on the screen looked like ants crawling on a wall. There were hundreds of them, but they didn't mean anything.

After a half hour of writing, I erased everything I'd written and started pacing around the room.

The day's events had made me nervous and edgy, but at the same time they had pulled me from the stupor I'd been in. There was no doubt that the experience had been completely different from anything I had ever gone through.

I had never rescued a beautiful princess before.

I woke up in front of a dying fire in the living room. All the wood had burned, leaving only bright embers and glowing coals.

I stood up, and my shoulder painfully chastised me for the position in which I had fallen asleep. I went to the bedroom to check on Ana Laura.

The room was warm and cozy. She was breathing evenly, and when I touched her forehead, I was relieved to find that she didn't have a fever. It was five A.M. so I got undressed, threw a couple large logs on the fire, and got into bed. . . .

. . . I got to the bottom of the well, but Ana Laura wasn't there. The floor was dry clay, and the heat inside was unbearable.

I tried to climb back out, but I couldn't. Every time I climbed up a step, the ladder sank farther and farther.

Finally, it stopped sinking and I ascended, but when I got to the top of the ladder, even stretching my arms as far as I could reach, I was still more than three feet from the rim of the well.

I looked right in front of me and saw a perfect rectangle cut into the side of the well. It looked like the entrance to a passageway.

I tried to push it, but it wouldn't budge, so I took out my Swiss Army knife and stuck it in the crack. It was definitely a separate piece of stone from the rest of the wall, about two feet square. I was certain that it was the entrance to the cellar.

Excitedly, I called Ana Laura several times, but she didn't answer my calls. I kept calling. "Ana Lauraaaa . . . ! Ana Lauraaaaa . . . !"

When I opened my eyes, Ana Laura was very close to my face, shaking me and softly saying, "Wake up. You're dreaming. Wake up."

I focused my eyes. It was already light outside, and she was wearing jeans and a camel-hair sweater. She was beautiful.

"Is it over?" she asked maternally.

"Yes, I think so."

"What were you dreaming about?"

As I described my dream, her mouth opened in surprise. "The entrance exists," she said excitedly. "Exactly as you described it. That's what I was doing yesterday, when I lost my balance and fell into the well."

We decided to go into town and buy the things we would need to explore what we both thought would be the entrance to the cellar.

On the way I confessed to Ana Laura that I had had the same nightmare she had two nights ago.

She was quiet for a few minutes and finally spoke. "That means that there is something down there waiting for us. The dreams we've been having are only a vibration. A signal."

There wasn't a real hardware store in town, but we found a large, old-fashioned general store where you could pick up anything from caramels to the latest model gasoline generator.

We bought three high-powered flashlights and a lot of batteries, a twelve-foot aluminum ladder, a pick, a blowtorch, a shovel, a maul, a hammer, two stone chisels, and snow boots for both Ana Laura and myself.

Ana Laura paid for everything on her credit card. I promised to reimburse her when the stories I was working on were published, but she made a gesture indicating that it didn't matter. It seemed she was completely convinced that we would find more than enough in the cellar to cover the expense.

We loaded the car and tied the ladder on top as best we could. Then we drove back to the house.

"How do you feel?" I asked Ana Laura in the car.

"I have butterflies in my stomach."

She didn't have to elaborate. I felt the same.

After we put on our new snow boots, the first thing we did was take a look at the well.

From above, even in the light of day, you couldn't clearly see the cutout section in the wall. You had to look very carefully even to imagine it. The old ladder from the attic looked like something dead inside the well.

We carried the aluminum ladder and the rest of the equipment over to the well and started working.

We heated the rungs of the ladder to a glowing red with the blowtorch and lowered it. There was a hissing and a thin column of steam when it came into contact with the frozen water at the bottom of the well. We pressed it down, and it sank a little farther. It seemed secure, so I descended and lifted up the wooden ladder from the night before. Ana Laura lifted the top as it emerged, and we removed it from the well. We loaded up with the rest of the equipment, and Ana Laura followed me down into the well. The sun was at its zenith, so we figured we wouldn't have to use artificial light for the first two hours.

Just as in my dream, I descended the ladder to about three feet below the rim and found myself even with the opening. I used my knife to see whether there really was a separation between the concave rectangle and the rest of the wall, which was covered with a thin layer of clay.

"What do you see? Can you move it?"

"No, not yet. Hand me the maul."

I gave it a couple of sharp whacks, but it didn't move, only made a hollow sound.

"Let me try," Ana Laura commanded impatiently.

I stepped aside and lit a cigarette while she climbed quickly to the level of the opening with the maul in her hand and started swinging wildly at the rectangle.

Fifteen minutes later and soaked with sweat, she climbed down to where I stood, disillusioned.

"We could try chipping the stone," I suggested.

"With one hand? That pick must weigh at least twenty pounds."

I climbed up again, this time with no tool. If it really was an entrance, there must be some way to open it. Bernabeu wouldn't have gone to so much trouble for no reason.

"Give me the hammer."

I hit all the surrounding stones one by one.

Nothing.

I climbed down, and Ana Laura took my place on the ladder, pressing stone after stone over and over, with no result.

Half an hour later, exhausted and depressed, we climbed out of the well.

Back inside the house, we took a couple of beers out of the refrigerator. Ana Laura paced in front of the fireplace with a can of Heineken, her eyes glued to the floor. I was happy just to watch her. She was a goddess, there was no doubt.

She stopped suddenly. "Let's be logical. If you were Bernabeu, where would you put the button, lever, or whatever it is that opened the door?"

I made a gesture of impotence with my hands. "I don't know," I replied stupidly.

"Think!" she ordered.

She finished her beer and crushed the can with her hands.

"If it's the entrance to his hiding place"—I noticed that Ana Laura spoke about it with doubt for the first time—"then the release mechanism has to be somewhere easy to reach but not noticeable to others." She paused. "We've been wasting our time miserably," she said.

"Why do you say that?" I asked, not knowing what else to say.

"Can you imagine Bernabeu inside the well with a hammer? He would have wanted immediate access to his hiding place. Let's go to the well!"

And with that, she ran out of the house and I followed along behind her.

Out at the well again, Ana Laura felt delicately around the edge, then searched the stone arch. She had run her fingers around nearly half of the arch, then stepped down and moved to the other side to continue her exploration. Suddenly, her face lit up. "There's something here!" she shouted.

I moved closer to see what she had found. Near the bottom of the arch there was a separation between two stones. It wasn't very large—Ana Laura's fingers barely fit.

She poked around for a few seconds in the hole, and we heard a sharp *click,* followed by the grinding sound of rocks rubbing together.

We lowered ourselves into the well, where the rectangular stone was slowly moving. There it was, the dark but clearly outlined entrance to a tunnel.

Ana Laura was so excited she almost lost her balance on the ladder.

"We did it! We did it! See? I told you we'd do it. What do you think?"

"Let's see," I said cautiously.

I looked into the opening. It really was a tunnel, darker than a bear's cave and equally disturbing, but there it was.

"What is it?"

"A tunnel."

"Let me see," she said, climbing down the ladder and pushing me farther down.

"Hand me the flashlight."

I passed her the flashlight, and the next thing I knew this beautiful woman already had half of her body inside the opening. Then I heard her voice, echoing, "Follow me."

If I had had sufficient time to speak rationally with her, I would have discussed the possibility of how best to enter the tunnel properly equipped. After all, it was a nasty hole, and we would probably find the things one usually finds in holes: rats, spiders, maybe a snake. But Ana Laura's attitude demanded action, so a few minutes later I found myself crawling along the tight passageway, illuminating Ana Laura's rear end as she charged on fearlessly.

It occurred to me that Bernabeu might not have left the entrance to his hiding place so easily within reach—anyone's reach. There could be an endless array of devices meant to prevent the advance of the enemy inside the narrow tunnel.

Suddenly I was overcome with paranoia and tried to communicate it to my partner, but she didn't even stop to listen to me.

"Shut up and keep following me," she said sharply.

So I did.

After about thirty feet, the tunnel ended. We found ourselves in a space that was larger than the passageway, about five feet square. The only possible way to continue was through a wooden panel on the far wall, more or less the diameter of the tunnel through which we had just come.

There was a bar across the panel, and Ana Laura tried to remove it, but it was too heavy. I took the bar, pulling with all my strength, and the panel opened with a loud cracking sound.

Ana Laura shone her flashlight into the opening and immediately commenced her descent.

"Ana Laura!" I shouted. "Wait! You don't know what you're going to find down there."

She didn't bother to answer me and continued her descent.

I stayed, cowardly, at the entrance to this new tunnel, not daring to follow her. "What's down there?" I ventured.

"Another tunnel."

I followed Ana Laura—as usual—and we advanced along the new passageway. This one was only about ten feet long. We came to another open space, much larger than the previous one and ending at a door about five and a half feet tall. The door was metal, just like the one in my first dream.

Ana Laura moved aside so I could try to open the door. I pounded it fiercely with the maul. The sound echoed against the tunnel walls, but the damned door wouldn't budge. I pressed the weight of my body against it several times in vain; I was going to have to break it, which would be impossible with just the maul. We agreed to climb back up to the surface—the clean surface—to decide what to do next.

Something had seemed strange inside the tunnels, but I couldn't quite put my finger on it. However, once outside, I knew exactly what it was. We hadn't found any spiderwebs along the way, much less mice or rats, which indicated that the stone we had opened in the wall of the well had completely sealed off the air supply to the tunnels.

It was too late to go into town for tools we could use to break down the door, so we got undressed and spent the rest of the afternoon making love all over the house.

We were both in a wonderful mood, since we had made such an intriguing discovery. The next day, one way or another, we were going to get past that door and uncover Bernabeu's secrets—and we hoped, his treasure.

The next morning we left the house at ten o'clock to go into town. We were very nervous and excited, like Oscar nominees feel on the night of the awards.

The store was almost deserted.

The shopkeeper greeted us without enthusiasm, even though we were probably his first customers of the day.

"We need an electric saw, a hundred-yard extension cord, an electric drill and metal drill bits, and some saw blades."

The guy looked at us for a couple of seconds, as if we had ordered a pizza with anchovies, instead of merchandise that he handled every day.

He moved about the store until he had gathered everything we had asked for.

Ana Laura used her American Express card again. I have never seen her as happy as she was when she signed the charge slip. That was an indication of her emotional state—of our emotional state.

Neither of us spoke on the way back to the house.

When we arrived, we unloaded the car and went into the house for a few minutes to warm up and to steel ourselves for the task ahead.

Ana Laura lit a cigarette and breathed in the smoke deeply, then stood up and went into the kitchen. When she returned she had the bottle of Fin vodka and two glasses. She sat on the sofa. "Get ready," she said. "We're about to begin the most extraordinary adventure of our lives."

She poured two glasses, and we toasted solemnly.

After finishing our drinks, we connected one end of the extension cord to an outlet in the kitchen and went out into the cold to meet our destiny.

Then we lowered ourselves into the well and, holding the flashlights in one hand, sort of crawled through the tunnel. As we advanced, unrolling the extension cord, I imagined all sorts of things awaiting us, from an enormous treasure in gold and silver coins to the appearance of a giant rat weighing fifty pounds, or a vicious spider. The place didn't lend itself to much else.

I was tempted to suggest that we should forget about the whole thing and get out of there, but I didn't want to sound like a chicken.

When we reached the metal door—the one that had been in my dream—at the end of the second tunnel, I switched on the drill and easily perforated the metal. When I removed the drill bit from the hole, I felt something very disconcerting. A tiny current of air was sucked into the space on the other side of the door. It reminded me of what happens when a vacuum-packed can of preserves is opened. I made a few more holes while Ana Laura shone her flashlight on the work area.

When there was a large enough opening in the door to insert the saw blade, the tunnel began to fill with a nauseating odor.

"It smells like death," declared Ana Laura.

In different circumstances the comment would have been nothing more than a simple assemblage of words. But, echoed several yards underground, it made every hair on my body stand on end and sent an ugly chill through my bones.

I vacillated for a minute, but Ana Laura urged me on.

"Hurry up, I don't want to spend all day down here."

I introduced the saw blade into the holes I had drilled in the metal door and turned on the saw.

If the drill had produced an unsettling noise, it was nothing compared with this. The metal yielded easily, but the vibration and the noise were unbearable. When I had cut about thirty inches, I stopped. My hands were sweating profusely and trembling uncontrollably.

Ana Laura took my place and grabbed the saw. "Shine the light on the saw!" she ordered.

And I did, trying to control my shaking hands.

The beautiful girl had a better disposition but not the strength for a job like that, so after ten or fifteen inches, she, too, was sweating and turned off the saw.

The air had gotten very thin from a lack of oxygen. I suggested that we climb back out for some fresh air, but she refused. "Let's finish, there's not much left," she said, handing me the saw.

We were trying to cut a rectangle, and more than half of the work remained undone, so I continued.

Soon the smell of death had completely invaded the tunnel, and my stomach churned with intermittent nausea. My head was splitting from the noise.

Finally—just as I thought I was about to vomit—the door yielded with a loud creaking noise.

With a sharp kick I pushed it in.

Although we both had wanted to reach that moment for several days, we stood there paralyzed.

Neither one of us made a move to enter the newly opened space for several seconds. Finally, Ana Laura took the initiative and shone her light inside.

"You're not going to believe it," she said, clearly surprised.

"What's in there?"

"Come on, you're just not going to believe your eyes." Having said this, she stepped through the opening in the door.

What I saw when I followed her left me with my mouth open.

We were in a cellar exactly like the one in each of our nightmares during that night before we started our search.

But that wasn't the only surprise of the day.

The air inside the hiding place was wretched. It was as if we had opened a tomb. And, without realizing it, that's exactly what we had done.

It didn't take us long to realize that we had made a truly macabre discovery.

The cellar felt very familiar because of our dream. The burlap bags of walnuts, hazelnuts, and pine nuts were there, as were the boxes of dried meat, the crackers, and the jars of preserves.

But something that hadn't appeared in the dream and was indeed present here was a pair of cadavers, sort of mummified, one beside the other on the floor.

We stood there hypnotized, looking at the human remains.

Despite the fetid odor, the lack of air, and the horrible scene, Ana Laura maintained an enviable composure.

"What do we do now?" I asked, trying to breathe as little as possible.

Ana Laura cupped a hand over her nose and mouth.

When she answered my question, her voice sounded appropriate to the situation. It seemed almost like a voice from the other side of the grave. "Let's get out of here."

We exited the tunnels as if the two cadavers were pursuing us.

I had never been so thankful to see the light of day as I was at that moment.

Once outside, we breathed deeply for a few minutes before speaking.

"Let's get in the house!" Ana Laura finally said.

The first thing we did was to take a shower in an attempt at disinfection. The second, of course, was to sit with a few glasses of vodka in front of the fireplace in the living room.

"What do we do now?" I asked, breaking the silence.

Ana Laura ruminated for a few minutes before replying.

"Basically, we have two options. If we call the police, the rental agency could accuse us of damaging their property. The contract clearly states that we can't make any modifications to the house without prior authorization—in writing—by the agency. Besides, anything of value that we find would automatically belong to them. All our trouble would have been for nothing, and, even worse, we would have to pay for the damage.

"The other option is to look for anything of value, get it out of there, close up the passageway, and leave as if nothing had ever happened here."

The idea of going back down into the improvised tomb put an ugly knot in my stomach. But there was something else. I had never imagined that Ana Laura would be so ambitious as to dare something like returning to that eerie cellar.

She seemed to guess my thoughts. "The bodies down there must be Bernabeu and his wife," she said. "And they must have been there for more than a century. I don't think it will bother them if we look for a little compensation for our efforts. Do you?"

"No, I don't suppose so. But I don't think I can stand that smell for very long."

"Here's what we'll do. Tomorrow we'll go into town and buy a couple of those masks that painters and carpenters use. That'll make it a little more bearable. You'll see!"

She stood up and took me by the hand. "Meanwhile, let's make sure the time slips by in the most pleasant way possible," she said happily as she guided me to the bedroom.

Ana Laura undressed and got into bed, making a coquettish signal for me to join her.

Thanks to the exhaustion induced by breaking into the hiding place and our passionate sexual activity, we slept peacefully.

Never before had I enjoyed her body and her caresses as much. It was as if she were a condemned woman enjoying her last pleasure.

The next morning, we got up early and went to town to buy the masks. Again, the shopkeeper looked at us suspiciously. He seemed to be imagining what we could be doing at Bernabeu's house. I didn't like the guy at all.

We quickly returned to the house and got to work.

The putrid air in the cellar had dissipated a bit, and there was now only a peculiar smell like that of dead rats.

Wearing the masks, we worked in stages. First we looked around for a while, then we left again to breathe fresh air. Of course, we didn't know exactly what we were looking for. Since the cadavers were near the door and were in the way, I decided to move them, barely overcoming the feeling of nausea.

The body we supposed was Bernabeu's disintegrated as if it were made of cardboard, and I ended up with a large bone in my hand.

Using a stick, I moved his companion's body, which also pulverized upon contact. I piled the remains of both in a corner and covered them with a blanket.

Then I went out to breathe fresh air. Ana Laura followed me.

It was a particularly cold day, but the temperature in the cellar was pleasant.

After the third trip through the odious tunnels, Ana Laura made a discovery.

She had accidentally torn the bag containing the pine nuts and discovered that it was nearly half full of gold coins. Ana Laura immediately tore the other two bags and found they too contained gold coins. It was a fortune! My beautiful companion began to laugh and shout hysterically, the sound reverberating eerily against the walls of the hiding place, even through the masks. We put a few coins in our pockets and went back out through the tunnels.

We went into the house since it was already late afternoon and we needed time to plan the easiest way to remove our treasure.

After taking a long, steamy bath, we settled in front of the fire with sandwiches and a bottle of white wine.

Ana Laura was euphoric and couldn't stop talking. "I told you. I told you. Didn't I? Do you know how many coins there are down there? There must be a few thousand, and they're enormous," she said as she admired the large coin she held in her hand.

She sighed with happiness.

"We have to get them out of there and leave this place as soon as possible."

I agreed.

Though the discovery of the treasure had put me in a terrific mood, I was not at all pleased to have to be constantly returning to the cellar. Somehow I felt as if we were robbing a grave.

The temperature had plummeted and we were spent, so we went right to bed.

Just before falling asleep, I heard my beloved's happy voice, "I told you. Wow! I told you. . . ."

It had snowed all night, and the next day we had great difficulty in reaching the well. At the bottom there was a black stain. It was a dead bird. A crow. Ana Laura paid it no attention, and we began our work, only this time the tunnels were even more slippery and inhospitable than ever. After the third trip, just as we were about to finish the job, I felt a presence behind me. It couldn't have been Ana Laura, because she was on the other side of the room. Frightened, I turned around and nearly jumped out of my skin when I saw Bernabeu standing in the doorway to the hiding place.

I barely managed a terrified shout.
"Ana Laura . . . !"

I woke up shaking and sweating. Ana Laura was looking at me as if I were crazy. There was concern in her face.

"What happened?" she asked in a shaky voice.

"Nothing. I had a nightmare. That's all."

She left the bedroom and returned with a couple of glasses and the bottle of vodka.

She filled both glasses to the rim and drank half of hers in one gulp. I did the same.

"What was your dream about?" she asked.

"It was stupid," I assured her, now that I was fully awake and felt sure of myself.

"What was your dream about?" she insisted.

I described my nightmare, and she emptied the rest of her glass in one swallow. Then she took a deep breath.

"It's not possible. I just had the same dream. You woke me up when you called my name. I was just turning around in my dream to look at the door to the hiding place."

Since I couldn't think of anything sensible to say, I, too, emptied the contents of my glass.

It was almost dawn, so we didn't even bother going back to sleep.

A lot of ideas were bouncing around inside my head and, undoubtedly, in Ana Laura's. Up to that point, our dreams had been closely linked to real events. The cellar was exactly as we had dreamed, and so was the access to it through the well.

Ana Laura hadn't spoken since we got out of bed and was now preparing our breakfast.

"What do you think about the dream?" I asked.

"Telepathy. We've been together for a long time, and lately we've been isolated from the rest of the world. I'm not surprised that we can communicate telepathically."

"I agree," I said. "But so far our dreams seem to have a lot in common with reality."

"Javier, please! Bernabeu must be dead over a hundred years now. You don't think he's coming back to claim his money, do you?"

"It could be a premonition."

"Premonition or not," declared my beautiful Ana Laura, "we're going to get all of those damned coins out of there. So let's hurry up and get it over with as soon as possible."

After breakfast, we returned to the well. It was a pretty cold day, but I was relieved when we discovered that it hadn't snowed during the night.

We got to work filling two small suitcases. The first trips to the cellar were relatively simple, but as we repeated the operation, our fatigue mounted since the tunnels were becoming humid with our breath, making the way increasingly treacherous. By noon we had managed only to empty one of the bags and we were completely exhausted. Not even the thought of all that gold could motivate us to keep going, so we loaded the coins in the trunk of the Volkswagen. We struggled to finish in the slippery snow. Finally we finished and went inside. We took a long bath and then lay in front of the fireplace devouring mouthfuls of smoked turkey. We didn't speak much, partly because we were so tired, and partly because somehow the business in the cellar had distanced us from each other.

Ana Laura didn't say so, but I felt that she considered me

less of a man than before. And I, at the same time, had discovered that the carefree, bohemian girl I once new had become ambitious and was capable of doing anything to get what she wanted.

"What are you thinking about?" she asked.

"About us. It seems like all this has damaged the great relationship we had."

She was quiet for a few minutes before she spoke.

"I don't see how one thing has anything to do with the other. Relationships change, and ours is no exception."

Then she took my hand and led me to the bedroom, where we made love furiously.

Fortunately, there were no dreams that night.

We woke up well into the morning and repeated the work of the previous day. Our lovemaking the night before not only hadn't helped bring us closer together, but in a certain way had distanced us even more.

At one point I had imagined that Ana Laura was only trying to please me sexually, without caring about me as she had before. It was almost as if sex were just a way of keeping us together until we finished the job.

In my eyes this made her nothing more than a whore. A very beautiful one, but a whore just the same. And, even worse, when we found ourselves at the peak of our lovemaking, I was more turned on thinking of her in that way.

How could a couple change so much in such a short amount of time?

We stopped working at five that afternoon, put the coins

in the Volkswagen with the rest, and went into the house. After a steaming bath and dinner, we caressed each other in front of the fire in a preamble to the night of sex awaiting us. We were both terribly excited.

Once in bed, upon contemplating Ana Laura's lithe body, I fantasized about her being a beautiful prostitute.

We made love savagely. I possessed her roughly, as if I had paid for her body, and I was surprised when she responded enthusiastically. It was sex without love. Animalistic sex.

A few minutes after we finished, Ana Laura was fast asleep. I couldn't sleep. I felt at odds with myself. I couldn't understand how a few gold coins could destroy my real treasure, which was this woman.

I went to the kitchen and poured myself a glass of vodka and then another and another.

I turned the thought over and over in my head. Maybe Ana Laura had changed so much that she would leave me once we returned to the city. Or worse, her ambition could go further. Why divide between two? Once the coins were loaded in the Volkswagen, what would prevent her from getting rid of me?

Was she capable of something like that? Was that what our latest dream had meant? Was it a premonition?

I returned to the bedroom and still had difficulty falling asleep.

The sky was dark when we woke up the next morning. I went to the kitchen to make coffee and saw through the window that it had snowed during the night.

Getting to the well was even more difficult than before, and when I looked down at the bottom, my blood froze. There was a black stain in the snow. I hurriedly climbed down the ladder behind Ana Laura and shivered violently when I saw that it was what I had feared: a dead crow.

She was already halfway inside the tunnel when I shouted. "Wait a minute."

"What?"

"What do you mean 'what?' Don't you see? It snowed all night, like in the dream. A dead crow in the bottom of the well!"

"So what? You're not afraid of ghosts, are you?"

"No, but . . ."

"If you don't want to come down, don't. Wait for me in the house. I'm tired of your cowardice."

She turned around and headed deeper into the tunnel.

I went back into the house and found a sharp knife, which I hid in my clothing. Premonition or not, whatever happened, I wasn't going to be surprised without a weapon.

The tunnels seemed more slippery than ever, and somehow the smell of death had become accentuated, penetrating the masks.

We made several trips in silence. When we were finished collecting the coins, my hand went instinctively to the knife. As we turned to leave, there he was, just like in the dream.

Only it wasn't a ghost. It was the man from the store in town where we had bought all our equipment.

He had a powerful flashlight in one hand and a large pistol in the other.

"You finally finished? City rats are different from country rats, as far as I can see. Okay, let's see what you found."

"What we found doesn't concern you," said Ana Laura haughtily.

The man discharged his weapon into the roof of the cellar. The shot sounded like a cannon firing inside the tiny space.

Ana Laura and I quickly opened the suitcase we had just filled with coins.

The beam from his flashlight illuminated the golden contents.

"My God!" he exclaimed. "That damned Bernabeu had some money, didn't he?"

"Yes, he did." Ana Laura spoke gently. "But there's enough for everyone. You take this suitcase and we'll take the other one and we'll call it even."

"City rats are definitely different. Why should I have to share anything with you when I can take it all myself?"

"Then take it and leave us in peace."

"I will leave you in peace, that's for sure. I have no option. You understand that I can't leave you alive. It wouldn't allow me to enjoy my fortune."

Then the bastard pointed his weapon at my head.

"Wait!" shouted Ana Laura. "This isn't all the gold."

"Oh really?"

The man aimed his flashlight at Ana Laura's face. Then, suddenly, I pulled out the knife and, in a surge of anger, cleanly slashed the aggressor's throat.

More dead than alive, he managed to shoot into the air a couple of times, but he didn't hit anything. Then he fell forward, his flashlight making a macabre play of light on the walls and ceiling of the cellar.

He was still quivering when Ana Laura leaned over him.

"He's dead," she said coldly. "Let's get out of here!" she said, grabbing a suitcase full of gold coins.

It was too much for me to take in. I had just committed homicide and my companion was acting as if we had only killed a spider. However, as if hypnotized, I took the other suitcase and followed her through the tunnels.

Outside it had started snowing again, and we made our last trip to the car.

Once inside the house, I felt completely numb—and not just from the cold. Ana Laura poured a couple glasses of brandy, which we drank in silence.

Finally, she spoke.

"How do you feel?"

Curiously, I felt as if everything had taken place onstage. Everything seemed completely unreal, as if it were just one long nightmare, from which I would wake up any minute.

I refrained from answering her and instead asked, "What are we going to do now?"

"Simple, we'll close up the entrance to the cellar and leave everything just as we found it."

"We're not going to call the police?"

"Of course not! No one knows about that hiding place, so no one will come looking for that man out there. We'll wait a few days so they don't connect us with his disappearance, and then we'll go."

This was definitely not the sensitive and humane woman who had arrived with me at this damned house. Ana Laura had changed.

But when I really thought about it, the man had earned his

punishment. He had threatened us and had even pointed his gun at me, surely ready to shoot.

If we notified the police, I would be accused of murder and Ana Laura of being an accomplice. We would lose the money and our freedom. In a small town like this, we were sure to be condemned. It was enough just thinking about a jury of people like the hateful librarian to know what the verdict would be.

Ana Laura was right. There was no other choice. It was best to let a few days pass, then hit the road.

Suddenly, I had a paranoid thought. Was the man really dead?

Gathering up my courage, I decided to go back and see.

"Where are you going?"

"To the cellar. I want to make sure he's really dead."

"That's not necessary. I . . ."

Without letting her finish, I left the house and walked toward the well.

This time the tunnels held the smell of fresh death. When I arrived at the hiding place I confirmed with relief that my victim was indeed dead. A large pool of blood had formed around his head.

I was about to leave when the photograph of Bernabeu and his wife caught my attention. For some reason, I took it with me.

When I exited the first tunnel, I put the wooden panel back in place, and once I reached the well, I closed the opening in the stone wall. Last, I removed the aluminum ladder and carried it to the house.

I spent the rest of the afternoon and part of the night getting drunk, trying to forget the ghastly sensation of cutting a man's throat.

The next morning we went straight to the store in town. An elderly man was behind the counter. We bought what we needed to repair the attic ladder and reattach it.

Everything in town was as it had been before, except for the absence of the shopkeeper.

Ana Laura paid for our purchases, and we returned to the house.

The Volkswagen was noticeably heavier, but we still managed to climb the steep hills.

As the days passed, the image of the killing was gradually erased from my memory. But I had become obsessed with the fact that Bernabeu and his wife had died inside their refuge. So, as Ana Laura had done earlier, I spent hours studying the notebook of drawings, trying to find the answer.

Curiously, Ana Laura began to finish the work she had been neglecting. Our roles had been reversed.

I remembered clearly feeling a vacuum when I perforated the metal door, which led me to believe that Bernabeu and his wife had died of asphyxiation, having breathed all the air in the small space. This led me to two questions: first, why hadn't he been able to open the door to the hiding place, and, second, if the cellar had been designed to hide people for prolonged periods, why didn't it have adequate ventilation?

After turning it over and over in my mind, I arrived at the conclusion that the entrance from the well wasn't the main entrance to the hiding place; there must have been another entrance. Logically, it would be much more accessible than the well.

In addition to the drawings, I studied at length Bernabeu's wedding picture, as if it held a clue. I became so obsessed that the homicide and the gold lost their importance. My relationship with Ana Laura had dissolved completely. One day, while we ate dinner, she asked, "What are you planning to do with your half of the money?"

The idea had never crossed my mind. Until that moment I had thought of us in terms of a couple, not individuals.

"I don't know," I replied, and then asked, "How about you?"

"The first thing I'll do is take a long vacation. The beaches in the south, I think."

"Alone?"

She noted the disappointment in my voice and quickly continued. "Look, Javier, all relationships need to breathe to get stronger."

I knew that it was all over. This relationship didn't need to breathe, because it couldn't breathe anymore. It was dead.

Two weeks after the incident, the homicide, we decided to leave. We packed up the Volkswagen. Fortunately, the return trip would be mostly downhill; otherwise, the tiny car wouldn't have been able to make it.

I put out the fires in both fireplaces, and we were about to leave when a thought occurred to me. The only place we hadn't looked for access to the cellar had been the fireplaces.

I thoroughly cleaned the floor of the fireplace in the living room with a brush and found what I had suspected. Looking carefully, one could see a thin line separating the block of bricks in the center from those on the periphery.

Surely Bernabeu had descended to his refuge with his wife, confident that everything would function well. Somehow, the entrance had sealed hermetically. It didn't matter because there was the entrance from the well. But Bernabeu hadn't taken into consideration the fact that the house would settle with time, so that when he tried to open the metal door leading to the tunnels, he couldn't.

The man had died in a terrible way, in the very refuge he had built to escape death.

I took the photograph, the notebook of drawings, and the architectural plans for the house with me. I was sure no one would miss them since they had lain abandoned so long in the attic.

In order not to give the impression that we were fleeing, we stopped in the town and went to Guillermo's café.

The bartender recognized us immediately and sat with us, bringing his glass of brandy with him.

"How's the work going?" he asked in an agreeable tone.

"We've finished," replied Ana Laura. "In fact, we came in to say good-bye."

"Good, I hope you have a nice trip home and that you come back soon."

He drank his brandy in one gulp and returned to his place behind the bar.

When we left he accompanied us to the car.

Ana Laura gave the old man a kiss on the cheek and climbed into the vehicle. As I was about to get in, Guillermo took me gently by the arm and asked me in a low voice, "Was it worth it?"

"I beg your pardon?"

Guillermo smiled genially and winked.

Needless to say, we never went back there.

The coins ended up being worth much more than Ana Laura had calculated, since besides being solid gold, they were very old. A man from Thailand bought the whole lot, no questions asked.

Ana Laura took off as soon as she had her share of the money, and I haven't heard from her since.

The plans for Bernabeu's house are now beautifully framed and hang prominently on the wall in my studio. The wedding photograph is on my desk.

I anonymously sent the notebook of drawings—much later—to the town library.

After all, the town's treasures couldn't be trusted in the hands of "people like us."

NEIGHBORS

The path of excess leads to the tower of wisdom.

—WILLIAM BLAKE

THE LOTZANO family had saved for many years to buy a condominium in one of the best parts of the city.

They had always been a very close-knit family: Señor Lotzano, his distinguished wife, their older son, and two young, working daughters, twenty and twenty-one years old.

Señor Lotzano prided himself on his respectable family name and had always been an upright man. He had never smoked; he didn't drink; and since he had married Lucila when he was twenty-one, he had never had relations with another woman.

Fidel, at twenty-three the eldest, was an exact replica of his father. He had dated the same girl for two years and meant to marry her as soon as he finished his studies at the National University. Patricia was twenty, pretty, and a virgin. She was from a good family, with an unquestionable background.

The two Lotzano daughters, Purísima and Virgen, did not have boyfriends. They viewed dating as a preamble to marriage and did not want to waste time or risk the family's good name on pointless adventures.

Señor Lotzano did not have a university degree, but he had been employed for twenty-five years at a foundry. Having started as a worker in the ovens, he now he held the estimable position of subdirector of production and was the union treasurer. He thought that when he reached sixty he would retire with a good pension and enjoy the calm life of a man who has never done anyone any harm.

However, when they moved to the home of their dreams, the Lotzanos had not taken into consideration that they would have to share the building with several neighbors, especially those such as the Casquivan family upstairs.

There were five people in the Casquivan family, that is, if they could be called a family.

Señor Casquivan had been married four times; his current lady friend was really his mistress, since he didn't have the money to settle his last divorce and had decided that a free union was better. He was fifty-five but looked like he was eighty. Shaky and invariably reeking of alcohol and tobacco, he shared his condo with his three children, products of his first two marriages. Viviana, the oldest, was twenty-four and had already had two abortions. She was an attractive woman with brilliant green eyes and only two objectives in life: to have a lot of money and to have a good time. Until now she had achieved only the latter. Her brother, Adonis, was twenty-two and had spent half of his life in one of the best schools in the world: a correctional institution. Though his specialty was breaking and entering, lately he had branched out into pyramid schemes and raffles with nonexistent prizes, with which

he earned enough to support his vices. Deseo, the youngest,
was a handsome blond with blue eyes. Women invariably turned
to look at him. He lived by his body and was currently studying architecture at a private university, thanks to a grant the
dean had given him in exchange for certain favors that she had
never quite spelled out. Tita, Señor Casquivan's mistress, was a
thin, attractive woman who had worked as a waitress in a bar
for many years and had finally ended up a prostitute. That's
how she met Casquivan, who was captivated by her innocent
looks. Now, at twenty-eight, she had a more or less tranquil
life. At least she could sleep at night like other people.

That was the family that fate had determined would be the
Lotzanos' new neighbors.

The Lotzanos finished moving in on a Saturday afternoon.
Following proper custom, as they always did, they decided to
visit all of their neighbors in the building, spending a little time
with each family. Since there were only six units, they thought
there would be enough time on Sunday to begin their neigh-
borly duty, so when they returned from nine o'clock mass,
they started to make their rounds on the first floor.

That's where they were first alerted to the evil lurking on
the fifth floor. The father was a good-for-nothing. The sons
were a pair of wild playboys. Señora Tita was a nice woman.
Viviana was a very active woman. Too active.

The Lotzanos had led sheltered lives and didn't pay any
attention to the warnings of their neighbors on the first floor.

No one was home on the second floor, and on the third
floor there was a bitter woman who practically threw them out

of her apartment as soon as they finished introducing themselves.

Their neighbors on the fourth floor were a recently wed couple who had been living in the building for a only few months and were moving soon since the husband, who was an engineer, had been offered a job in Tijuana.

The Lotzanos arrived at the Casquivans' door on the fifth floor at eleven-thirty in the morning.

Señora Tita opened the door wrapped in a sheer robe, left over from her days as a cocktail waitress. She invited them in and offered them beer, which the Lotzanos politely refused, as well as the shots of tequila, an empty bottle of which sat in the middle of a cluttered dining room table. Finally the parents accepted a cup of coffee, and their offspring settled for soft drinks.

They had barely begun their introductions when Adonis appeared in the dining room. He was wearing tight jeans and a white T-shirt that announced, "I hate everything." He quickly surveyed the two young women and arrived at the conclusion that they were silly girls and most likely still virgins. He left the room, promising to go down to the Lotzanos' apartment later to offer them positions in his pyramid.

Tita, whose body was not at all concealed by the robe, excused Señor Casquivan, saying he had an atrocious hangover. In fact, she had just been preparing him some really spicy chilaquiles.

The Lotzanos soon began to feel uncomfortable and said their good-byes. Tita thanked them for their thoughtfulness and said not to hesitate to call her if they needed anything. Any little thing at all. The Casquivans were there to help.

That was the first time they met.

★ ★ ★

On Wednesday evening, as Señor Lotzano sat at the dinner table, enjoying some rolls and beans with a cup of café con leche, the doorbell rang, and moments later an old man appeared before him, preceded by a ghastly odor of alcohol.

"My dear neighbor," said the man in a slurred voice, "I have come to return the favor you paid my family on Sunday."

Extending a trembling hand, he added, "I am Señor Casquivan, or rather, what is left of him." He emitted a loud guffaw, and his breath violently struck Señor Lotzano's face.

"It's a pleasure," Lotzano said, as he felt his dinner making pirouettes in his stomach.

Casquivan took a seat without being invited and proceeded to pull out a flask, from which he took a of couple swigs, then extended it to his neighbor. Lotzano declined with a shake of his head as he said, "That's very kind of you, thank you. I don't drink."

"Never?"

"Never."

"You're smart. Liquor is bad for you, that's why I've decided to get rid of it all."

He laughed loudly again and took another gulp from his flask before returning it to the pocket in his jacket.

"I was about to eat dinner, would you care to join me?"

"What are you having?"

"Something light. A roll and coffee. But if you'd like we could make you something."

"Like what?"

Lotzano was beginning to feel uncomfortable. "I don't know. Maybe some meat."

"A steak?"

"No, meatballs."

Casquivan thought about it for a few seconds and then shook his head as he said, "Don't bother, friend, I really only stopped by to welcome you and to see if you needed anything."

Then he stood up and walked to the door, followed by Lotzano, who silently thanked God.

When Casquivan reached the door, he turned to Lotzano. "Do you happen to have change for a hundred?" he asked.

Lotzano put his hand in his pocket and took out a handful of bills, which he counted, then he shook his head.

"No, I only have sixty."

In a move worthy of a magician, Casquivan grabbed the bills from his neighbor's hand and said, "Then lend them to me, I'll send one of my sons down later to pay you back."

He left Lotzano standing with his mouth open.

Señor Lotzano ate a roll without relish and immediately began to feel stomach pains.

One morning, Purísima entered the elevator on her way to work and bumped into Adonis, who was coming in from a night of partying. His eyes were red from smoking marijuana, and he was wearing a T-shirt that said, "Fuck you."

"Good morning," said Purísima.

"Where are you going so early?"

"To work."

"At this hour?"

"It's almost eight o'clock."

"That's what I mean, it's barely light out. What do you do?"

"I'm a receptionist at a clinic."

Adonis looked appreciatively at the girl. She was wearing a tailored suit and was perfectly groomed. Maybe because of the cannabis, he had a sudden urge to go to bed with her.

"Well, have fun," he said in parting. "By the way, your watch looks pretty worn out. I'll sell you a couple of tickets for a Rolex raffle."

"No, but thanks anyway. I never buy raffle tickets."

Adonis stuck his hand in his pants pocket and took out two white cards with printed numbers.

"Which number do you want?"

"No. Really. Besides, you must excuse me. I'll be late for work."

"What about thirteen?"

"Really—"

"I'll put you down for thirteen and thirty-one. What's your name?"

"I really—"

"I've already put you down. I can't erase you now; it would ruin the list and change everybody else's luck."

Adonis's voice sounded convincing and soothing. Purísima started to imagine herself wearing the Rolex on her delicate wrist.

"Purísima."

Adonis raised his eyebrows exaggeratedly.

"Purísima? No, seriously, what's your name?"

The girl opened her bag and took out her identification card, showing it to Adonis.

He read the name and couldn't help smiling, revealing white, even teeth and conquering Purísima in the process.

Adonis wrote her name beside the numbers.

"Since you're new in the building, I'll only charge you for one ticket."

"Thank you!"

"It's a hundred."

"A *hundred?*"

"The watch is worth at least seven thousand."

Adonis gave her a look of superiority, which made her capitulate. Purísima put her hand in her bag and took out a checkbook. She wrote a check to "cash" for a hundred pesos and gave it to him.

Adonis took the slip of paper and rewarded her with another smile before turning to walk away.

"See you soon, Purísima."

"See you soon, Adonis."

As she emerged onto the street, it dawned on Purísima that she hadn't asked about the date of the raffle and was surprised when she realized she didn't care. The boy was incredibly attractive, and besides, he had given her a free ticket.

Of course, Casquivan never returned Señor Lotzano's sixty pesos, but every time the old man saw him, he greeted him enthusiastically as if they had been neighbors their entire lives. One night they arrived at the building at the same time. Casquivan, as usual, reeked of alcohol.

"My dear friend Lotzano. How are you?"

"Fine, just fine." Lotzano moved his hand protectively to his wallet.

"And your family?"

"They're fine too, thank you. Are you coming from work?"

"Yes, in a manner of speaking. I spent the afternoon working on a very pretty little number." Casquivan emitted one of his annoying laughs.

The comment didn't seem funny to Lotzano, who remained silent.

Casquivan went on. "You can come along any time you'd like. It's not exactly what you would call a bordello, but there are some cute girls that you wouldn't believe. And not at all expensive."

Lotzano couldn't believe his ears. Prostitutes? Were they talking about prostitutes?

"No, thank you. I never go with prostitutes."

"Never?"

"Never."

"You're right. Whores are the worst. That's why I try to wear them out until I give them a heart attack."

Casquivan erupted in a fit of bawdy laughter just as the elevator stopped at the fourth floor.

"Good night," said Lotzano.

"Night. By the way, what are you having for dinner? Something light?"

"Yes," Lotzano replied, and out of habit he added, "Would you care to join us?"

Casquivan immediately accepted. They entered the apartment at nine o'clock, and Casquivan didn't leave until midnight, when Lotzano and Lucila could no longer stifle their yawning. Of course, Casquivan dominated the conversation and managed to polish off an entire bottle of brandy.

The next day, Virgen was standing on a corner waiting for a taxi when a red sports car stopped in front of her. "Where're you going?" asked the driver, a gorgeous blond boy.

Under normal circumstances, Virgen would have ignored him, but he was so good looking she couldn't stop looking at him.

"I'm waiting for someone."

"At this hour? Come on, I'll give you a ride."

Virgen felt as if she were being hypnotized, and before she realized it, she was standing next to the car.

The boy extended a well-manicured hand. "Deseo Casquivan. It's a pleasure to meet you."

The last name set off an alarm in the young woman's brain. "Casquivan? Do you live around here?"

"Yes, why?"

"Is your mother named Tita?"

"She's not my mother. How do you know her?"

"We're neighbors." Virgen reached out her hand. "Virgen Lotzano."

He gently pressed the girl's smooth hand. "I've never known a virgin."

She smiled. The boy was really handsome.

"What a great car!"

"It belongs to a friend, but it's at your disposal. Are you going to school?"

"No, to work. You?"

"I'm on my way to the university. I'm studying architecture."

The boy's voice was very slow and guttural. Virgen felt a stirring in her groin.

"It's not out of your way?"

"Not at all. Where're you going?"

"To General Motors."

"It's on the way," Deseo lied.

They talked as they drove, and by the time Virgen got out of the car in front of GM, she had fallen completely in love with the boy. She suddenly felt terribly lonely as she watched him drive off.

Tita Casquivan was carrying two heavy bags, and as she approached the front door of her building, one of them tore open, scattering cans of beer everywhere.

Luckily, Fidel Lotzano appeared just then. "Allow me to help you, señora."

"Thank you, neighbor."

Tita was a woman who thought ahead. Since Señor Casquivan had been out all evening, she assumed he would come home with a terrible headache and demand beer.

Fidel helped Tita put the beer in the refrigerator and then turned to go. "I'll see you later, señora."

"Wait a minute, Fidel. At least have a beer or a soda."

Fidel accepted a Coca-Cola, more out of courtesy than anything else.

The young Lotzano boy was not overly attractive, but he

was strong and muscular, the type of man Tita had always liked. She lived with Casquivan because doing so gave her a measure of security and a home and family, but sexually the man was disgusting. He always smelled of alcohol, and every day it was harder for him to achieve an erection.

Tita found herself wanting Fidel as she watched him drink his soda. She was certain she could drive him crazy sexually. Her years of being a prostitute hadn't been completely in vain; she knew quite a bit about the art of exciting a man.

Fidel saw that he was being studied and began to feel uncomfortable. Señora Casquivan wasn't bad looking. He couldn't understand how she could be married to that old drunk. He could see that she was much younger than her husband. She didn't look more than thirty.

The silence became embarrassing, so Tita broke it. "What sports do you play, Fidel?"

"Karate, señora."

Almost without realizing it, Tita put a hand on Fidel's bicep. "You're so strong."

He tensed, but not because the woman's hand bothered him. Just the opposite.

Fidel finished the rest of his drink and said good-bye.

Tita accompanied him to the door. "You're always welcome here. Come up anytime you want."

"Thank you, señora."

"I'm not that much older than you. Call me Tita."

"Okay. See you later, Tita."

* * *

Señor Lotzano became extremely cautious regarding Casquivan. Especially after the night he and his wife had suffered through the interminable stories about his vile womanizing. Now, each time Lotzano approached the building, he looked around to make sure Casquivan wasn't in the vicinity. One night as he was checking to see if the coast was clear, Lotzano heard a woman's voice behind him.

"Are you looking for something?"

Maybe it was his surprise, or the sensuality of the voice, but he felt a shiver on his neck. He turned and saw a beautiful young woman scrutinizing him distrustfully. Without knowing why, Lotzano felt guilty. "Excuse me?"

"I said, Are you looking for something?"

"No. Good evening. I live in this building, and I have a neighbor who's a pain in the neck. Before I go in I always check to make sure he isn't anywhere around."

"What's he like?"

"He's unmistakable. You can smell the alcohol on his breath from three yards away, and his laugh is unbearable."

"Are you the new neighbor?"

The woman's voice penetrated Lotzano's brain to its very core. She had a gorgeous face and was tall and thin. Lotzano realized that it had been a long time since he had looked at a woman like this. "Excuse me?"

"Are you the new neighbor?"

"Yes. How do you do? I am Señor Lotzano."

She looked him up and down, evaluating him, and finally extended her hand. "Viviana Casquivan. And don't worry, my father's not around. You're safe."

She turned and walked away.

Lotzano turned to stone as he watched her. He put his hand to his nose; the woman's perfume was delicious.

Deseo thought the neighbor had seemed nice, and he was attracted by her timidity. He had never really dealt with an immaculate woman before. From a young age, he had been the victim of seduction by his teachers, his parents' friends, and even a cousin from Monterrey who was ten years older than he. All of these women were voracious foxes, so the exchange with his neighbor had surprised him and he had begun to like her.

He took her to General Motors several more times, and one morning he said good-bye with a light kiss on the cheek, which caused her to turn red and become very nervous.

Virgen had felt Deseo fused into her brain and her heart from their very first encounter. Just thinking about him made her stomach ache, and she had begun to lose weight. Her parents grew worried, so her mother took her to the doctor, but he didn't find anything wrong medically. Nonetheless, she was sick. Sick with love.

One afternoon, Deseo invited her to a movie. She was already twenty, but she still asked her parents' permission, which was vehemently withheld. Señor Lotzano was especially opposed to it. He imagined that, with such a whoremonger for a father, the son must be one too. That sort of thing was in the blood.

"No, hija. I forbid you to go out with that boy. He's a terrible influence on you."

"But you don't even know him, Papá."

"I know his father, and that's enough."

Virgen didn't argue, but she was crushed. It was her first chance to go out with the boy she loved, and her father was trying to prevent her. It wasn't fair.

She had never disobeyed her father, but that afternoon, when Señor Lotzano went back to work, Virgen went to the movies with Deseo.

Of course, Deseo did not love her at all. He was just curious. In the darkened theater, he put his arm around the girl's shoulders. Far from rejecting him, she was very pleased. He didn't make any other advances, but that had been enough. Virgen had never been so happy.

The afternoon passed quickly, and Deseo invited her to a bar for a drink. She had completely forgotten about her father, but even if she had happened to remember, it wouldn't have mattered a bit. She was desperately in love with the blond boy, and she wouldn't give up being with him for anything in the world.

When Lotzano got home from work, his rolls and refried beans were already waiting for him, but he noticed Virgen's absence immediately and, in a fit of anger, went up to the fifth floor to look for her.

In his haste, he forgot his manners and pounded heavily on the Casquivans' door with his fist. He was about to pound again when the door opened and Lotzano's anger magically disappeared.

Viviana was standing before him, looking at him as if he were an enormous cockroach. If Lotzano had been captivated by her beauty the night of their first encounter in the dim light of the street, this time he was left breathless. In daylight, the girl was a monument to beauty. Her emerald eyes contrasted with her jet-black hair. Her lips were impossibly sensual, and her disdainful attitude only made her more attractive. And if that weren't enough, she was wearing an oversize white T-shirt, perfectly outlining the voluptuous curves of her body, most notably her firm breasts.

"Yes?"

"Goo–Good evening."

Viviana looked at him haughtily, saying nothing.

Lotzano tried to regain his composure and was making an enormous effort to move his eyes away from the girl's voluminous chest.

"Excuse me. Do you remember me? I'm your neighbor."

The woman nodded her head indifferently. "My father's not home."

"Uh, right, of course. I was looking for your brother, not your father."

"Nobody's home. When Adonis gets home, I'll tell him you were here."

Then, without saying another word, she started to close the door.

Lotzano prevented her. "Excuse me. I'm looking for Deseo, not Adonis."

The woman kept looking at him as if he didn't exist. "I already told you, nobody's home. If I see Deseo, I'll tell him you were looking for him. Good night."

Viviana nearly closed the door on Lotzano's nose, and left him feeling utterly ridiculous. He went back down to his apartment and discovered that he had completely lost his appetite. And not because of his daughter.

When Virgen came home, she was prepared for a serious

reprimand, but she didn't care. Having spent the evening with Deseo was worth any punishment in the world. But her father was sitting in front of the television with a dazed look on his face.

"Papá?"

Lotzano didn't stir.

"Papá, are you all right?"

"Eh?"

"Are you all right?"

"Yes. Yes, I'm fine. I was just thinking."

"Papá, I'm sorry I disobeyed you, but I have to confess that I'm madly in love with that boy."

Lotzano was far away.

"Papá, are you listening to me?"

Lotzano turned to look at his daughter. "Excuse me?"

"I said I love him, Papá. I'm crazy about him."

Virgen thought her father would react violently, but he didn't. He just nodded. "I understand, hija. I understand perfectly."

He didn't say anything else and stared off into space again.

Virgen kissed him tenderly on the forehead and went to bed. She wanted to fall asleep as soon as possible so she could dream about her new love.

Adonis and two of his accomplices broke into a house in a wealthy neighborhood one Sunday afternoon. It had been a long time since they had done that, but pyramid sales and raffle tickets weren't bringing in enough money. Especially with the high prices of marijuana and cocaine.

They found no resistance and easily subdued the two servants. In the master bedroom Adonis found a large amount of jewelry. They left quickly. It was a fast, clean hit.

They divided the spoils that same night. Each one was going to sell his own part; that way it would be harder for the police to trace the stuff.

As he smoked a joint and played with his share of the loot, Adonis had an idea. Among the stolen items was a women's gold Rolex in perfect condition.

The next morning he got up practically before dawn—almost eight o'clock—to intercept Purísima.

Adonis pretended the encounter was accidental. "Oh yeah, by the way, the winning number was thirteen," he said as he was about to walk away from her. He put his hand in his pocket and pulled out the watch.

Purísima couldn't believe it. She opened her mouth, but she didn't know what to say, so she closed it again. Very naturally, Adonis took the girl's left hand, removed the watch she had been wearing, and ceremoniously placed the Rolex on her wrist.

"I'll see you, Purísima," he said as he walked away.

She could only nod her head in silence.

As the days passed, Señor Lotzano realized he was completely obsessed with Viviana. His productivity at work started to drop. His wife began to seem much less important to him, and he spent hours on end with a blank stare on his face, thinking about that beautiful face and those gorgeous breasts. He wondered about the size and color of her nipples and thought about how sweet and exciting they must taste. He dreamed about walking down the street with a woman like that who everybody would turn to look at.

One day he locked himself in his office and masturbated thinking about what it would feel like to make love to Viviana.

When he penetrated his wife in their darkened bedroom, he fantasized that his neighbor was in bed with him.

Desperate, he spoke to his priest about the matter, but that didn't help much.

"My son, this is a test that God puts us through. You have always been an honorable man. Just try not to think about her. We are flesh and suffer the weaknesses of the flesh, but your soul is clean and healthy. Get that woman out of your head. Give yourself over to God!"

That afternoon Lotzano arrived at the building the same time Viviana did. She was wearing a black Lycra miniskirt and a white, nearly transparent blouse.

Not only did Lotzano not give himself over to God but he completely forgot about His existence. He felt a tightening in his stomach and hurried to catch up with the woman.

Luckily the elevator was stopped on the sixth floor, giving him a few minutes to enjoy the object of his adoration.

"Good evening."

Viviana looked at him as if he were an ugly wad of mucus. "What's so good about it?"

The girl's answer rattled him, and he began to feel ridiculous. To make matters worse, he noticed she wasn't wearing a bra and he could see her breasts through her blouse. Lotzano's legs started to tremble.

"Do you have a problem, Viviana?"

"What does it matter to you?"

"Well . . . uh . . . we're neighbors, aren't we?"

The girl lit a cigarette and blew the smoke in Lotzano's face. But far from taking it as an insult, he somehow thought of it as a caress.

"I don't have *a* problem; I have a *lot* of problems, but none that you can solve," Viviana said.

"Such as?"

She stared impatiently at the wall panel, which indicated that the elevator was still stopped on the sixth floor. "My boyfriend just told me to go to hell."

Lotzano was dumbfounded and, without thinking, exclaimed: "He must be absolutely crazy!"

"Yes. And he's a son of a bitch. Now, if you don't mind, I don't feel like chatting. Okay?"

Lotzano felt the urge to embrace her tenderly. "Viviana, please listen to me!"

She dismissed him with a look. "Now what?"

"I just want to tell you that whenever you have a problem, I am always ready to listen. I want to be your friend."

"I already have all the friends I need."

At that moment the elevator door opened, and they entered.

Lotzano knew he was acting like an idiot. He knew it, but he didn't care. The goddess had him trapped in her nets. When they arrived at the fourth floor, he said good-bye to her, noticing that the girl's nipples were enormous.

"I'm very sorry about your boyfriend."

She made a gesture of disgust.

"Good night, Viviana. And, please, let me know if there's anything I can do. Anything at all. I am at your service."

The beauty didn't answer but instead repeatedly pressed the button to close the elevator door.

Lotzano entered his apartment and went straight to the bathroom, ignoring his rolls and beans, and proceeded to masturbate.

Every time Purísima looked at the Rolex, she would think about Adonis. At first she'd thought the raffle had been a ruse to trick her out of a hundred pesos, and she had already forgiven him. But when he gave her the watch, she felt terrible. How could I have doubted him? She chastised herself.

One evening they arrived at the front door to the building at the same time. She was coming from a funeral and was very depressed. A friend from work had died in an automobile accident.

Adonis noticed the girl's sadness and took advantage of the moment. He invited her to a bar for a drink.

"I don't drink."

"This time you do. You need it."

Purísima coughed and felt her throat burn when she swallowed the brandy, but with the second glass she had to admit that she felt completely revived.

She looked great. Black suited her, and she wasn't wearing any makeup. Adonis wanted her even more.

They had another drink and walked back to the building. Her depression had disappeared and Purísima felt wonderful with Adonis at her side. At the door to her apartment, he kissed her on the cheek, and she suddenly hugged him and kissed him on the mouth. Adonis didn't want to push his luck and abstained from caressing her body. He simply kissed her delicately on the mouth. "I'll see you, Purísima."

"I'll see you, Adonis."

When she entered the apartment, her father was—as had been his habit of late—lost in front of the television. Purísima was afraid he would detect the smell of alcohol, but she quickly realized he wouldn't notice anything. Not even a circus elephant parading through the apartment. She gave him a wide berth, and Señor Lotzano didn't even blink. He was completely gone. Purísima went into the bathroom, then undressed and put on her pajamas. She wasn't tired, but she wanted to fall asleep as quickly as possible. She wanted to enter the dreamworld with Adonis next to her. The last thing she did was look at the phosphorescent face of her new Rolex in the darkened room.

Señor Casquivan took a swig from his flask and settled in to watch the fourth race of the afternoon. Although his luck had left much to desire in the first three, when it was time to place his bet for the next one, he had a premonition. As he was about to say the numbers three and eight, his tongued twisted and instead he said one and two.

As he left the betting window, reason told him he had been foolish. The combination he had chosen couldn't win. Horse number one, Yellow Lightning, hadn't won a single race in the last two months, and number two, Explosion, had badly lost his last twelve races; nevertheless, deep inside, Casquivan felt he would win.

"And they're off!"

Casquivan watched the horses run as if in slow motion. For the first time in his long life as a bettor, he could hear the hooves on the ground, the agitated respiration of the animals, and their riders' shouts. He felt the mounting tension in the crowd.

"Coming around the first turn is number four, Catrin, followed closely by number eight, Pegasus."

Casquivan squeezed the piece of paper tightly in his hand.

"Pulling up from behind is number one, Yellow Lightning, making a stupendous run."

Casquivan began to feel a cold sweat on his forehead. He was entranced.

"Coming around from the outside is number two, Explosion."

Casquivan felt a strong pressure in his chest as he watched horses number one and two advance along the track at a high speed.

"The contest is between Yellow Lightning and Explosion. They are leading by more than two lengths."

Casquivan felt as if he were floating.

"And they cross the finish line. First place, number one, Yellow Lightning; second place, Explosion. Race winners: one and two. One and two."

Casquivan clearly felt his heart stop. Without letting go of the winning ticket, he collapsed heavily onto the ground.

* * *

Tita made use of Fidel's muscles to help Casquivan up to his apartment. After a week in the hospital, he was going to have to use a wheelchair for a while.

Fidel was happy to help. Tita and he had become good friends, and he had spent time with her almost every day when she returned from the hospital. The poor woman was very lonely.

Once Casquivan was settled in his bedroom, Tita closed the door and sat in the living room, inviting Fidel to join her.

"No, I don't think that would be wise."

"Please, Fidel. Stay a minute."

Even though he was in good shape, the exertion had made him sweat. His shirt was open, and soon, Tita was caressing his sweaty chest.

They looked intensely into each other's eyes and merged in a passionate kiss that lasted almost a minute, at the end of which Fidel pulled violently away from Tita and stood up.

"I'm sorry, Tita! I don't know what I was doing . . . Forgive me! Please forgive me!"

In response, Tita took his hand and put it back on her body.

A few minutes later, with Casquivan asleep in his room, Fidel had his zipper open and Tita was working on him with her mouth, for old times' sake.

One Tuesday evening, Viviana arrived at the building in a particularly nasty mood. She had received a notice from the bank that left no room for misunderstanding: either she pay her past due balance, or the bank was going to repossess her car.

Señor Lotzano had been watching for her, and when he saw her, he approached. "Vivianita! How are you?"

"Shitty," answered the beautiful young woman.

Lotzano had never liked foul language, but whatever came out of that gorgeous mouth was welcome.

"But why?"

Viviana looked at him for a few seconds, as if she had just noticed his presence. "What does it matter to you?"

"It does matter, Vivianita. It matters more than you can imagine."

Viviana wasn't in the mood for ridiculous old men. "Go to hell!" she said.

"Calm down, Vivianita. Calm down. I beg you. What's your problem?"

The beautiful woman didn't respond. She had enough problems without having to deal with this idiot.

"Tell me, Vivianita!"

"Don't call me Vivianita."

"All right, Viviana, tell me. Maybe I can help you."

A light went off in some deep corner of Viviana's brain. "I don't think you can help."

"Try me."

The girl lit a cigarette and said, her words wrapped in smoke, "I need ten thousand pesos by tomorrow or the damned bank is going to take my car away."

"How awful, Vivianita! I mean, Viviana."

"You see? You can't help me."

Lotzano felt that this might be his only opportunity to establish a relationship with the woman of his dreams and, without thinking, said, "Of course I can! Ten thousand pesos, you said?"

She was about to answer "Yes, you old fool. What? Are you

deaf?" But her instinct told her that this man could be her sal-
vation, and, instead, she softened her tone. "That's right," she
said.

"Tomorrow afternoon you will have your ten thousand
pesos, Viviani—Viviana."

When she heard the magic words, the woman struggled to
give her best smile, as she said in a sweet voice: "But I need it
in the morning, before noon."

As he gazed at the girl's smile, Lotzano's spirit grew inside
him, soaring higher than ever before. "How about eleven
o'clock? Tell me where to meet you and I'll bring you the
money."

Viviana was thrilled. The old man was going to fix her
problem. She gave him the address, and Lotzano promised to
be there at eleven on the dot. They took the elevator up, and,
before saying good-bye on the fourth floor, Viviana took
Lotzano's hand. "You don't know how much I appreciate this."
Then she gave him a juicy kiss on the cheek and pressed the
button to close the door.

Lotzano almost ran to the bathroom, ignoring his wife, his
two daughters, the rolls and the refried beans.

She had kissed him!

Vivianita had kissed him!

Deseo wanted to do things perfectly, so he took Virgen to an
expensive restaurant, ordered champagne, and after they'd each
had a glass of the expensive liquid he said, "Virgen, do you
want to be my girlfriend?"

The girl almost fainted. Either she had heard incorrectly

or she was dreaming. She couldn't speak for a few seconds and finally got out the word with difficulty, "What?"

"I asked you if you want to be my girlfriend."

She nodded vehemently.

During the meal, she was like a kid with a new toy. She could barely pry her hand off Deseo's, and she gazed at him longingly. She felt like a princess in a child's story, with her handsome prince beside her.

Deseo had known for a long time that the girl was completely in love with him. She wasn't very tall, but she had a well-formed body and a sweet face. Deseo was an expert in the sexual arts, but the possibility of possessing a virgin was very appealing to him. Besides, he liked her. She was different. This girl didn't touch his penis through his pants or whisper obscenities in his ear. She didn't wear miniskirts with no underwear, or high heels. He imagined himself deflowering her completely: her mouth, her breasts, her vagina, her anus. Everything. To be the first in everything. To be stamped on her skin forever.

She, on the other hand, dreamed of marrying him. Starting a nice family with the man who had unleashed such passion in her soul. She would be the envy of all her friends. Deseo was a hunk, not just handsome or good looking. His physical perfection always attracted attention. One night, Virgen had dreamed that she had gone to bed with him.

After they left the restaurant, while they were waiting for the car, Deseo hugged his girlfriend and kissed her on the mouth. Softly at first, then increasing the intensity.

She was happy to let him do it. His tongue played with her lips, then her tongue. It caressed her teeth and the roof of her mouth. He softly bit her virgin lips.

When he finished, Virgen was in another world, another dimension. It had been her first kiss, and she was wet between the legs.

That night she went to bed in a delirium.

Her boyfriend!

Deseo was her boyfriend and she was his girlfriend!

Lucila Lotzano knew that something was wrong with her family. Her husband was in a constant state of unconsciousness. Her son had suddenly broken up with his girlfriend, with no explanation. Purísima frequently came home smelling of alcohol, and Virgen was walking a couple of inches off the ground.

And all this had happened since they had moved into the new building.

Although she firmly believed in God, she began to think someone had cast a spell on her family.

Purísima's taste for alcohol was growing in proportion with her feelings for Adonis. The man was so thoughtful and kind. He showed disdain for anything that Purísima didn't like. He wasn't afraid of anyone or anything, and there was no situation he couldn't handle.

Purísima knew she was falling in love with Adonis. He was on her mind all day. She remembered his jokes, his witty responses to her comments, and she admired how he handled things. She adored his smile.

And the gifts. Adonis had given her a beautiful gold bracelet and a diamond ring. When she looked at these things, she felt as if she carried her man wherever she went.

They went to a bar near the building, playing darts while they drank and talking with the other regulars, many of whom were Adonis's friends. It was a fairly heterogeneous but interesting group. Purísima was discovering that there was another world out there, beyond the safe little world her parents had created around her and her siblings.

Gradually she was learning that life wasn't as pure and holy as her parents had taught her. She realized that the absolute lack of vices was as bad as total debauchery. Everything was good as long as it was kept in balance. But abstaining from everything made a person into a strange creature in a world where things happened in a different way.

Alcohol, for example. From the first day she had tried it, she noticed that it allowed her to shed a lot of her inhibitions, which was not bad but, really, very good. That was how she had kissed Adonis for the first time, and in the same manner—under the effects of the elixir—she had allowed him to caress her breasts one night, in the doorway of their building. And it had surprised her that she had let him without any opposition at all, but his hands were magic, so soft and delicate, so delicious.

Purísima was changing her beliefs about religion. And she had good reasons for the change. How could it be wrong for a woman to let herself be caressed by the man she loved? Wasn't it humiliating to have to go confess before an old, fat man wrapped up in a cassock? Could there be a better way to worship God, our Creator, than by enjoying life?

Adonis had taken it upon himself to introduce and cultivate certain ideas in her mind.

"Sin?"

"If you touch me without being married, it's a sin."

"Do you like it?"

"Yes. I like it a lot. But it's not right."

"If you like it, it can't be wrong. God wouldn't create things that we like to touch and then forbid us to touch them, would he? In that case, God would be cruel and harsh."

"He's testing us."

"Why? He already knows how we'll act, doesn't he?"

Almost without realizing it, the young woman changed her beliefs: from God to Adonis, until one day he was everything and everything he said was the absolute truth.

As treasurer of the union, Lotzano was easily able to get Viviana's ten thousand pesos. He would replace the amount little by little, and, since he was trusted by everyone, his financial reports would be accepted without question.

Besides, what was ten thousand pesos in comparison with beautiful Viviana's happiness?

And the kiss. Hadn't it been worth it just for the kiss? When he gave her the money, Viviana had kissed him on the lips. It had lasted only a few seconds, but it represented all of life to him.

At that moment she had made him feel like a real man. Not the little caricature of a man he had been up until that point, but a macho man who rescued his woman from the worst dangers of the world and was duly compensated.

* * *

After tasting the fruit of love, Fidel had gotten bored with his girlfriend, whom he now considered a stupid pest.

Instead, he had gone crazy for Tita. The lithe woman had taught him things he had never imagined before. They rented a room in a nearby motel, and Tita expertly guided him in the diverse sexual arts.

He felt very masculine. After all, he was sleeping with an older woman, one who was married and incredibly wild in bed. He was proud of himself. He dreamed about working hard to free his woman from the grasp of the evil Casquivan, who had begun to organize poker games in his apartment but still couldn't go out.

Fidel's mother had tried to talk with him one night after he returned from an afternoon of lovemaking with Tita, and he had silenced her.

"I don't have anything to say to you, Mamá."

"But the way you broke up with Patricia isn't right, Fidel. That poor girl loves you and—"

Fidel had closed the door to his room in his mother's face. At first he felt guilty, but when he remembered Tita's round, white buttocks, he felt satisfied with himself.

Casquivan didn't seem bothered by his mistress's frequent absences. He knew there was another man in her life, but he didn't care. He was practical. If he, in the state in which he found himself after the heart attack, couldn't satisfy her sexually, it was natural that the young woman would look for satisfaction elsewhere. Besides, she continued to take adequate care of him, and she was very understanding of his needs. More like a daughter than a lover.

The card games he had organized had been a total success. Since he had nothing better to do, Casquivan spent his days handling the cards over and over until he became proficient.

He was making good money from poker in his own home, and not because he had such great luck, but because with the agility he had acquired in dealing the cards he could arrange them any way he chose, so he was guaranteed to win twenty-five percent of the games.

The time came when he felt well enough to go outside, but he preferred to pretend he was still too weak and took full advantage of the situation.

Viviana was fed up with the city and decided to go to Cancún for a few days. But she didn't have the money for the trip.

One night, she went down to Lotzano's apartment and knocked on his door.

When he opened the door, he was delightfully taken aback at the sight of his goddess. "Viviana, what a pleasant surprise!"

Without caring whether Señora Lotzano or any of his children were around, Viviana said, "Let's go out for a drink. Our apartment is full of smoke and poker players."

Lotzano was in his shirtsleeves and had loosened his tie. "Now?"

Viviana gave him her usual look of disgust and said, after exhaling in an exaggerated manner, "It's okay if you don't want to. I'll go by myself."

She had already turned to leave when he stopped her, taking her gently by the arm. "Give me a second, Viviani—Let me get my jacket."

Señora Lotzano watched him straighten his shirt and tie and put on his jacket, then asked him, "Where are you going at this hour?"

Lotzano had learned well from Viviana and responded haughtily, "What's it to you?"

"I'll tell you what it is to me! You're my husband!"

"Yes, unfortunately," he said as he walked out the door.

They went to the bar of a luxury hotel, where Viviana ordered a bottle of chilled champagne. Lotzano hesitated to drink, but fearing he would look ridiculous in front of this goddess, he ingested the bubbly liquid.

Half an hour later and with a second bottle uncorked, Lotzano felt like a superman. And for good reason. Viviana attracted the stares of all the other men in the room. With her legs crossed, she was practically displaying her gorgeous rear end, and her laugh filled the place with a lovely melody.

When Viviana saw that Lotzano was drunk, she cozily took his arm and, plastering her breasts against him, said, "You are so wonderful. You're a real man."

Lotzano already knew it. He felt so macho. He knew he was capable of pleasing any woman. In his haze of inebriation, he was certain that Viviana was crazy for him. Her warm breasts against his arm confirmed it. He was in heaven.

Viviana waited until the warmth of her body electrified Lotzano and then said, "You're going to say that I'm such a bother, but I have a little problem."

"What problem, Vivianita? With me near, you will never have any problems."

"I need some money."

Lotzano looked at her for a minute. Her black hair was adorably curly, and her green eyes shone as if illuminated from within by lightbulbs. And farther down, his arm brushed against the delicate fabric that contained the woman's enormous pink nipples. *His woman's.*

"Money's not a problem, Viviana."

"I just don't want to take advantage of you."

"Take advantage of me? I was born to serve you, darling. It's my only mission in life. How much do you need?"

At first, Viviana had thought that seven or eight thousand pesos would be enough for her trip, but considering the old man's disposition, she ventured, "Fifteen thousand pesos."

Lotzano's inebriation evaporated in a millisecond. *"Fifteen thousand pesos?"*

Viviana made a gesture of exquisite tenderness and, caressing her companion's nearly bald head, said in a little girl's voice, "If you can't to give it to me, I'll understand."

Her perfume made Lotzano even drunker than the champagne, and her hand caressing his head was much more than the good man could resist. Without stopping to think, he said in a hoarse voice, "You'll have the money the day after tomorrow."

Making an enormous effort to overcome her distaste, Viviana kissed him on the lips.

Purísima gave up her purity on a Friday night.

Adonis and she had spent the afternoon in a bar drinking. When they went out into the street, the air struck the girl's face like a slap, and she began to feel sick. So Adonis offered her something to make her feel better.

Protected in the doorway of a nearby house, the young man took out a little bottle half-filled with a white powder. He skillfully placed a bit of the powder on the nail of his little finger and put it under his girlfriend's nostril.

"Breathe in hard!"

Purísima hesitated a second and asked, "What is it?"

"Listen to me!" he ordered and repeated, "Breathe in hard!"

The girl obeyed.

The first thing she felt was a burning inside her nose, but in a few seconds it went away. Adonis took a little more cocaine on his fingernail and put it under Purísima's other nostril. She inhaled again, more confidently this time.

In less than a minute, the discomfort caused by the alcohol had completely disappeared and been replaced by an almost uncontainable euphoria.

Purísima had never felt so good. Without leaving the doorway, she kissed Adonis on the mouth several times, while his hands roamed over her body.

The girl realized that she was getting excited, but she didn't care. Nothing mattered. She felt *so good!*

Adonis's expert fingers slid beneath Purísima's skirt, and before she knew it they were under the elastic of her panties.

She didn't object. There was nothing wrong with that, was there? God wouldn't create things for us to touch and then forbid us to touch them, would he? Besides, if she liked it, it couldn't be bad.

When she felt Adonis's fingers massaging her clitoris,

Purísima forgot everything else and just enjoyed the feeling it gave her.

Adonis took her to a hotel down the street, drugging her again before undressing her.

Purísima felt incredibly good and was fully aroused.

Adonis had everything under control. He kissed and licked the girl's whole body, paying special attention to her small breasts and the region between her legs. When she was perfectly lubricated, he offered her another hit of cocaine, and he took a few himself. Afterward, he penetrated her delicately.

Purísima arrived home at almost two in the morning. She was euphoric. Her mother intercepted her, demanding an explanation for her late arrival. Purísima wasn't in the mood to give explanations.

"We'll talk tomorrow, Mamá."

"No. We'll talk right now! You smell of alcohol!"

"Tomorrow, Mamá." Then she shut the door to her room in Lucila Lotzano's surprised face.

Señor Lotzano's stomach felt strange. He had spent the morning adding up numbers over and over. Finally, at noon, he reconciled the figures, but his nervousness and feelings of guilt had played havoc with the digestion of his breakfast.

However, deep inside he felt terrific. He closed his eyes, and all he saw was Viviana's exquisite face. And her stupendous body. He felt like a schoolboy with his first love. Besides, wasn't he man enough for a woman like her? At fiftysomething, didn't he deserve a little pleasure in life? A little compensation for all his years of hard work?

He was convincing himself that there wouldn't be any problems. He would take care of putting the money back.

He kept telling himself there was nothing wrong with that attitude. He had never spent his money on women or vices. It was only fair that he could do it now, one way or another, wasn't it? And, too, all of this was very little indeed compared with the pleasure that Viviana's company provided him. Just looking at her made his legs tremble and his spirit soar. And just remembering the looks of envy from the other patrons of the bar made his worries disappear and filled him with a deep sense of pride.

Of course, a woman like that wasn't won easily. She had to be earned. A man had to demonstrate that he was sufficiently intelligent and capable. There weren't many Vivianas in the world, so one had to stretch to the maximum to reach her level.

And the kiss! In front of everyone. A long, tender kiss from a grateful woman.

"The hell with everything!" he said to himself. He would balance any account necessary to have that goddess.

"I want to make love to you," Virgen said boldly.

Deseo looked at the girl for a while. A lot of women had thrown themselves at him during his short life, but they had been meaningless adventures. Virgen, on the other hand, was a trophy of sorts in his collection.

He had caressed her several times, always being careful not

to get too close to any important areas. He had kissed her neck and her ears and kissed her mouth almost to the point of asphyxiating her, but he had never touched her legs or breasts. He wanted to deflower her once, one single time, and completely, not in parts.

The young woman had expressed her desire to marry him. Deseo pretended he wanted to marry her too but held her off, saying he was only twenty and he had two more years of school. It might be four years before he had enough saved to get married.

That was too long for Virgen to wait. The more she tried to control herself, the more she thought about making love with her boyfriend, her cherub.

The previous night she had dreamed that he had done certain things to her, and she had awakened with wet panties. She thought she had urinated. But no, it had been the elixir of love that had dampened her underwear.

Deseo had done a good job on her psychologically. In contrast to his brother, he had never influenced Virgen in her religious beliefs. He had encouraged her to remain pious and had even said he thought she should be a virgin when she got married.

Knowing women, Deseo knew that his suggestions would end up having the opposite effect. He knew instinctively that Virgen would become so obsessed with the idea that she would end up trying to convince him they didn't need to wait so long. Love is a sickness that clouds women's minds, and eventually they surrender, wedding or not.

And so there they were, in his red sports car. They had been passionately kissing, and Virgen had proposed what he had been expecting.

"Are you sure?"

"Yes, I want to give you all my love. I can't wait any longer."

"Are you absolutely certain?"

"Yes, my love. I want to be yours as soon as possible."

Deseo smiled inside.

Viviana returned from Cancún deliciously tanned. She had been there eight incredible days. Of course, she had spent every cent of the money that Lotzano had given her. But it had been worth it. She had gotten involved with a six-foot Canadian and had eaten, drunk, danced, and made love almost to the point of exploding. The vacation had been good for her.

Mindful of her gold mine, the first thing she did was visit Lotzano.

If she had been the most beautiful woman in the world to him before, she was now simply beyond comparison. Her green eyes stood out exquisitely from her bronzed skin, and she seemed happy and carefree. When he saw her, Lotzano immediately thought about the money he had taken from the union's savings account, and, far from feeling remorse, he congratulated himself for having done it. Seeing Viviana like this was worth every cent and even more.

Viviana greeted him warmly with a kiss on the cheek. Lotzano was alone in the apartment. His daughters had gone out, Fidel was in some hotel with Tita, and Señora Lotzano had gone to visit a sick friend in the hospital.

"Come in, Viviana. How was it?"

"Marvelous. Are you alone?"

"Yes."

"Perfect. I want to show you something."

She closed the apartment door behind her and without warning took off the white T-shirt she had been wearing.

Lotzano almost had a heart attack. Viviana's beautiful breasts spilled out only a few inches from his face. The large, pink nipples stood out from the white skin where a tiny bikini had blocked the tropical sun's rays. The rest of the woman's torso was very tan. The sight was sublimely erotic.

"What do you think?"

Lotzano's mouth was open, but he couldn't speak.

She gave him a coquettish look. "Do you want to see the rest?" she asked, like a naughty girl.

He barely managed to nod his assent, he was so hypnotized by her beauty.

Viviana casually took off her tight jeans. She wasn't wearing underwear, so in a fraction of a second she stood completely naked in front of the pleasantly surprised Lotzano.

She turned around like a professional model, and he admired the overwhelming beauty that nature had concentrated in her being.

Her dark pubic hair contrasted with her white skin and her tan line. When she turned, Lotzano thought he was dreaming. Viviana's slim buttocks were a white treasure, standing out starkly from her tan legs and back.

A few seconds later, she put her clothes back on and said good-bye to Lotzano, who had not been able to utter a single word. She kissed him on the cheek again and opened the door.

"Was it worth the expense?"

Lotzano nodded several times.

Viviana's perfume still floated in the air when Lotzano reached the bathroom and masturbated savagely.

Purísima left her job at the clinic and started doing something more lucrative. Adonis had set her up selling raffle tickets and pyramid schemes. The girl felt that she belonged to her man, body and soul. She felt like a slave, but the idea, instead of worrying her, pleased her enormously. Finally she had found her real reason for living: to serve her master.

Deseo didn't push Virgen. He had all the time in the world, and he wanted everything to be just right. He borrowed a house in the country from some friends.

Virgen told her parents—rather than asking for permission—that she was going away for the weekend. Her father didn't even pay attention to what she was saying. Her mother, however, resisted and began to interrogate her.

"Who are you going with?"

"A couple of girlfriends."

"Virgen, my God! You have never lied to me before! You're going with that blond upstairs, aren't you?"

"The blond upstairs has a name, Deseo. And no, I'm not going with him. I'm going with some friends from General Motors."

"Darling, please. Your father and brother and sister are bewitched. You are the only normal one left. Please don't do this to me!"

"I'm not doing anything to you, Mamá. I'm only going

away for the weekend with some of my girlfriends. What's wrong with that?"

"What friends? I want their names and telephone numbers."

"Why?"

"I want to make sure you're not lying to me."

"You don't trust me?"

"Yes, I do, but you must understand my situation. Strange things are going on around here. I feel like my family is disintegrating. I feel you running through my fingers. Please understand!"

Virgen knew what was waiting for her that weekend, and she soon tired of her mother's pleading. She wanted to be with the one she loved.

"I'm going, Mamá."

"No! I want the names and telephone numbers of those girls or you're not going anywhere!"

When she thought about the angel waiting for her in the red sports car, Virgen exploded. "I am not a little girl anymore. You can't tell me what I can or can't do. I'm an adult now, and you have no right to treat me like this. I am going. Besides, Papá already said I could go."

"Your papá is ill. Haven't you noticed?"

"Maybe you are the one who is ill, Mamá."

Señora Lotzano decided to use her strongest weapon. She started to cry.

Instead of moving Virgen, her mother's weeping only made her more impatient. "Enough, Mamá! Stop being so ridiculous. I'll see you Sunday night."

She turned and left Lucila Lotzano drowning in her impotent tears.

* * *

As they rode along the highway to the lake, Virgen felt as if she were in a fairy tale. The vegetation couldn't have been more lush and exuberant. Her prince drove the automobile as if it were a chariot. Deseo looked handsome in his sport clothes, and he was wearing a beret that made him even more attractive.

Along the way, in accordance with his plan, Deseo had played classical music, mainly Mozart. In order not to spoil the magic, they had spoken very little, but their fingers were intertwined and separated only when Deseo needed to control the car on a dangerous curve.

The house, too, was a dream. It was a rustic cabin but with all the modern conveniences.

Deseo lit a fire and chilled several bottles of champagne. He had bought pink Heidsieck for the occasion.

They began caressing each other around six, and by nine, after two bottles of champagne, Virgen was about to explode, so Deseo carried her to the bed.

He considered himself an expert, and with good reason, but he knew he had to take special precautions with a virgin. He wanted her to remember this day her whole life, especially the details.

He had planned to disrobe her bit by bit, as if she were a delicious caramel. But when he came back from the bathroom, Virgen had already undressed and was under the covers.

Deseo lit some candles and turned off the lights. He put on some soft music. The room looked like a scene from a painting.

He got into bed and started kissing the girl on the mouth while his hands explored the territory that now belonged to him unconditionally.

He was surprised to find that her breasts were large, larger than they appeared when she was dressed. And her buttocks were firm and smooth. He didn't remember ever feeling skin as delicate as Virgen's.

She had lost her nervousness, but she was still very excited. After caressing her for a while, Deseo stopped to pour more champagne.

Virgen looked beautiful by candlelight. The reflection of the flames in her eyes made Deseo think she looked like a beautiful witch, disguised as a virgin to trap him.

He kissed and licked the girl's sweet nipples and then sucked them hard, leaving them slightly bruised. He wanted her to remember him each time she looked in the mirror.

He moved down her body, kissing each part of her firm abdomen and her navel, until he reached her pubic hair. He spent more than a half hour kissing and licking her there. When Virgen was no longer simply enjoying the pleasure but shouting like a crazy woman, he introduced his penis into her virgin mouth and maneuvered them into a sixty-nine position.

The inexperienced woman hurt him a few times. He was driving her wild with his tongue, and she nearly bit his penis.

Once that part of the ritual was finished, Deseo delicately spread Virgen's legs, lifting them upward, to hurt her as little as possible.

She was perfectly lubricated, and what little pain she felt was exquisite.

He penetrated her slowly as he kissed her lips and neck to keep her excited. Once he was all the way in, he began to move rhythmically.

Virgen emitted groans of pain and moans of pleasure. She felt as if she were being reborn. Or better still, as if her life was beginning at that moment and everything before had been a dream.

She hurt a little, but she was happy. Deseo extracted his penis and tried to penetrate Virgen in her rectum. She became tense.

"No! Not there, darling! Not there!"

"Yes, my love. If I do it in the front I might get you pregnant."

"Get me pregnant! I want to have your child!"

"No, my love. Of course we'll have a child. And not just one, but not yet. We are too young and I don't want to ruin your life."

As he was saying this, he kept trying to invade Virgen's tightly closed anus.

She finally gave in to her love for the boy and relaxed a bit; then she felt her lover's penis rending her rectum.

The suffering didn't last long. In less than a minute, Deseo discharged all the desire he had built up over the past several months into his girlfriend's rectum. Then he withdrew and rewarded her with a long kiss on the mouth.

Virgen's pretty brown eyes were filled with tears of happiness and pain.

Viviana stopped in front of the window of a car dealership. The object of her attention was a white convertible.

She went inside.

Two salesmen fought for the pleasure of helping her. She

was wearing a miniskirt that perfectly displayed her firm thighs and a T-shirt that revealed her navel. On a less attractive woman, the outfit would have been somewhat vulgar, but it made Viviana look like a goddess.

She got into the car and started pressing all the buttons while the salesman stared at the beautiful legs in front of him.

"It's the latest model," he said, adding, "It was made just for a woman like you."

Viviana, who hadn't even acknowledged the man's existence, caressed the fine leather of the seats with her well-manicured hands and raised and lowered the power windows. She was like a child in a toy store.

"How much does it cost?"

"The list price is a hundred ninety-eight thousand, but taking into consideration that you would be a great advertisement for the car, and if you pay cash, we could let you have it for a hundred ninety."

Viviana stayed in the car for a few more minutes and then got out, showing every inch of her long legs as she did so.

"Hold it for me."

"With pleasure, señorita. How much of a deposit do you want to leave?"

Viviana dismissed the salesman with her look, and he agreed to take her name without again mentioning a deposit.

Viviana knew she would get the car. She remembered Lotzano's face the day she had disrobed in front of him, and she didn't doubt that the man would do anything to possess her. If she handled things right, he would give her the money.

But nothing in life is free. She would have to put up with the displeasure of going to bed with Lotzano; the convertible was well worth the sacrifice.

She knocked at his door on Saturday morning.

Lotzano opened the door as if greeting the Archangel of the Annunciation.

"Viviana! What a pleasant surprise!"

"Are you alone?"

"Yes."

"Can I come in?"

"Of course, Vivianita."

Fidel had gone to karate class, Virgen was at the proctologist's, and Purísima was out selling pyramids. Señora Lotzano was at the grocery store.

Viviana made a superhuman effort and kissed Lotzano on the lips, inserting her tongue in the man's bland mouth. Lotzano didn't waste any time and immediately grabbed hold of the diva's buttocks.

While she tried to avoid having to kiss him again, Viviana allowed Lotzano to fondle her as he wished, faking moans of pleasure.

After a few minutes, she opened her blouse and let him kiss her breasts, trying to focus her mind on something more pleasant.

Lotzano had imagined this scene a dozen times while he masturbated in his office or in the bathroom at home. Now his fantasy had materialized. He thought he was dreaming.

A few seconds later, Viviana took him by the hand and led him to the master bedroom.

She sat on the double bed and, with Lotzano standing in front of her, lowered his zipper and extracted his penis.

Lotzano was incredibly excited, but even so, the size of his member was ridiculous. Viviana closed her eyes and tried to think about something else as she took his penis into her mouth and expertly sucked it.

Lotzano couldn't believe what was happening. He caressed his lover's hair as he murmured incoherently. "Oh, Vivianita! Ay, my love! I love you, Viviana! My darling!"

In her entire life, Viviana had never dealt with a penis of such minuscule proportions, but when she thought he was ready, she lay on her stomach on the bed and raised her buttocks exaggeratedly, then lifted her miniskirt up around her waist. "Make me yours! I beg you! I want to feel you inside me!"

Lotzano couldn't believe his ears, and, fearing he would wake from his dream any minute, he aimed his minipenis at Viviana's vagina and swiftly penetrated her.

Viviana panted and moaned, feigning pleasure, while Lotzano pushed his tiny penis in and out of her ample vagina.

Because of Viviana's exaggerated panting, they didn't hear the apartment door open.

Unluckily for Señora Lotzano, she had forgotten her coupons and had come back to get them.

Drawn by the noise, Lucila Lotzano approached the bedroom as if hypnotized. When she witnessed the scene, her legs turned to rubber. She thought she was going to faint.

Meanwhile, with their backs to her, the two lovers copulated furiously.

Señora Lotzano felt infinitely ashamed and left the apartment without making a sound, heading for the street.

Viviana made the best of Lotzano's excitement. "You love me, don't you? Tell me that you love me!"

Holding the beautiful Venus's hips and sweating like a crazy man, Lotzano answered. "Of course I love you. I've loved you since the first time I saw you. I adore you!"

Between faked pants, Viviana went on. "How much do you love me?"

"Completely, my love. I love you all the way."

"Would you do anything for me?"

At that instant, Lotzano's little penis started to swell. He was about to ejaculate inside the woman of his dreams.

"Yes, my darling. I would do anything."

"Promise me!"

Lotzano's orgasm began just as he responded. "I promise you, my love! I promise you, darling! I would do anything for you! My love! My life! I love you!"

When Lotzano finished, Viviana quickly went into the bathroom and with great repugnance washed herself thoroughly.

She barked an order at Lotzano. "Get dressed! I want you to see something."

Lotzano was in another world. If at some moment he had thought he was in love with Viviana, that was nothing compared with how he felt after possessing her. His love for her was ten times greater now.

Like an automaton, he got dressed and left the building, his lover's hand in his.

"Look! Isn't it gorgeous?"

Lotzano looked at the automobile that Viviana had indicated.

"Very nice, but it must cost a fortune."

"Not at all. Only a hundred ninety thousand pesos. What do you think?"

At that moment, a cymbal crashed in Lotzano's head. "A hundred ninety thousand pesos is a lot of money, my darling."

"Let's go in! I want you to see how I look in it."

Viviana entered the showroom confidently and got in the car.

Lotzano's legs were trembling. Partly because of the sexual activity a few minutes before and partly because he was imagining what was about to happen.

"What do you think?" asked Viviana from inside the automobile.

"You look gorgeous!"

Viviana got out of the car and hugged Lotzano, whispering in his ear like a little girl. "Will you buy it for me? Tell me yes! Tell me yes!"

"Viviana, my love, I don't have a hundred ninety thousand pesos!"

She gave him a crushed look and walked out of the showroom without saying another word. He caught up with her at the door and tried to take her arm, but she brushed him off.

Lotzano tried to explain. "Viviana . . . I-I'm not a millionaire."

She looked at him with disgust. "You're shameful! First

you made me fall in love with you, and once you got what you wanted, you don't care about me anymore."

"Viviana, please! I love you! Believe me, if I had the money, I would buy you the car."

"You took advantage of me! You used me!"

"No, Viviana. I love you like crazy, believe me!"

"You're just like all the others. I'm only a toy for you. A sex toy. I don't want to see you ever again!"

Her acting was worthy of an Oscar. She left Lotzano standing in the street.

As he watched her go, he felt his heart breaking.

Señora Lotzano had watched Viviana and her husband leave the building. She still hadn't been able to digest what she had seen in her apartment. Her husband! In her room! In her bed!

Purísima immensely enjoyed each hit of cocaine, and if she liked it, it couldn't be bad, right?

One Saturday afternoon Adonis sent her to buy drugs.

At first she refused, but he easily convinced her. "They don't know you. You go, you get the stuff and give them the money, then you come back. That's it. Like going to buy cookies."

"I'm afraid."

"Do you think I would send you if it were risky? Do you think I would put you in danger?"

She tenderly caressed her lover's face with the back of her hand. "Of course not."

"Then go."

He told her where to go and who to ask for.

Purísima imagined that it would be a squalid lower-class neighborhood, but she was surprised when she arrived at a luxurious building.

She knocked at the door, and a man in his forties answered. "Yes?"

"El Pollo?"

"Who sent you?"

"Adonis."

"Come in."

The interior of the apartment was filled with antiques, tapestries, and paintings. Purísima didn't need to be an expert to know that they were real.

A younger man appeared.

"El Pollo?"

"Yes."

"Adonis sent me."

El Pollo took an envelope from his jacket and gave it to the girl.

She in return handed him a roll of bills. El Pollo counted them and put them in his jacket. Then he pulled out a small gold case and a tiny matching spoon. He opened the case and skillfully filled the spoon, carrying it to his nostril and inhaling quickly.

Purísima was in awe of the elegance with which one could take drugs.

El Pollo filled the spoon again and placed it beneath the girl's nostril. She inhaled deeply.

This cocaine was something different. The feeling in her

nose wasn't the same as she had experienced with Adonis's powders.

In a few seconds Purísima began to feel good. Extraordinarily good.

Soon she was overcome by giggling. First it took the form of small, broken laughs, then less interrupted laughter, and finally long fits that made her eyes tear.

El Pollo watched her with a wide grin on his face.

Purísima finally calmed down, and he filled the spoon again and passed it to the girl, who accepted it eagerly.

El Pollo invited her to sit down, and he poured her a glass of cognac.

As Purísima drank the cognac, she thought she couldn't remember ever drinking anything more delicious.

Time was gliding along pleasurably between glasses of cognac and spoonfuls of cocaine, with no words spoken. Only Purísima's laughter.

She didn't remember passing out, but when she opened her eyes, it was already morning. She was in a big bed, completely naked. When she tried to move, she felt a sharp pain in her rectum. Finally she was able to turn over, and what she saw almost made her vomit.

El Pollo and the man who had opened the door to the apartment were asleep, naked, embracing each other like a married couple.

Purísima got up with difficulty and looked for her clothing, which she found in the living room, where she had laughed most of the previous evening. Each time she took a step, she felt a sharp pain in her rectum.

She quickly dressed and fled the apartment.

★ ★ ★

Virgen was miserable. After she returned from the country, from the magical trip, Deseo had not come to visit her. He hadn't even called. It was as if he had been swallowed by the earth.

One night she went up to the fifth floor to look for him. She wanted an explanation. Especially now that she had given herself to him and she was more in love than ever.

Tita opened the door, revealing a haze of tobacco smoke and the noise of a poker game in progress.

"Good evening, señora."

"Hi!"

"Excuse me. Is Deseo home?"

"No, I haven't seen him for a few days. Let me ask his father where he is. Do you want to come in?"

"No, thank you. I'll wait here."

The seconds felt like an eternity to the lovelorn girl. Finally, Tita reappeared. "It seems that he went to San Antonio to buy some things. Casquivan says he doesn't know when he's coming back."

"Thank you, señora."

"You're welcome."

Virgen returned to her apartment, where her father was tallying and retallying numbers on a calculator. She locked herself in her room and cried inconsolably.

Viviana knew that Lotzano would end up buying her the car; it was just a question of time. After all, she had already let him